BRO BONES
TAPESTRY OF BLOOD

RON FORTIER

C000063022

AIRSHIP 27 PRODUCTIONS

Brother Bones: Tapestry of Blood
All stories © 2014 Ron Fortier

Brother Bones and all characters in this book are copyright solely by Ron Fortier.

"The Butcher's Festival" appeared in *The Pulptress* from Pro Se Productions (2012)
The Pulptress is copyright © Tommy Hancock-all rights reserved
"The Bruiser from Bavaria" appeared in *Pro Se Presents* #12 July 2012
"The Plastic Army" appeared in *Pro Se Presents* #19 Summer 2013

An Airship 27 Production
airship27.com
airship27hangar.com

Cover illustration © 2014 Patricio Carabjal
Interior illustrations © 2014 Rob Davis

Editor: Ron Fortier
Associate Editor: Roman Leary
Production and design by Rob Davis
Promotion and Marketing Manager: Michael Vance

All rights reserved under International and Pan-American Copyright Conventions. No part of this book may be reproduced in any manner without permission in writing from the copyright holder, except by a reviewer, who may quote brief passages in a review.

ISBN-13: 978-0692225813 (Airship 27)
ISBN-10: 0692225811

Printed in the United States of America

10 9 8 7 6 5 4 3 2 1

CONTENTS

THREADS : PROLOGUE

As a new sun began to creep over the sleeping port city of Cape Noire, a gypsy seer named Countess Selena sat in front of a linen covered table with her deck of Tarot cards. An incense burner filled the room with a sweet smell and through the half-open window behind her she could hear crows screeching at the hot rays of dawn.

"It's going to be an important day, dear Lord." She took the worn deck in her soft brown hands and began to shuffle them. "After the evil Dragon was defeated by Mister Bones and his friends, the city is beginning to stir again."

She started laying out the cards before her, familiar with each image and what they represented.

"Many, many people go about their affairs once again forgetting the horrors of the past few weeks. Streets and buildings are made clean and the refuse left behind is swept away so that they can forget."

Holding the deck with her left hand, she reached over to the half-filled glass of black rum and took a drink.

"But life is a cycle and with each new day, new threads are woven that will encompass so many; good and bad, saints and sinners."

She took one more drink to empty the glass. "And now, cards, show us the players in this new chapter that spreads out before us.

"Lord, have mercy."

☻ ☻ ☻

Young Billy Carpenter pedaled his red bicycle through the busy streets of downtown avoiding milk trucks, buses, taxis and early rising pedestrians as he raced along. It was Tuesday morning, his turn to serve as altar boy for Father O'Malley's seven a.m. mass. He had never been late before and wasn't about to start today. Never mind what the kindly old pastor would do if he were late; it was the wrath of his mother he feared the most. And so he wove his way through traffic and people, up one street and down another while Cape Noire came alive all around him.

He zipped past McClaren's Five & Dime and saw a woman in the front display window removing the dress from a female mannequin. At thirteen, the sight of naked breasts, even plastic ones, was enough to turn any boy's head. At the same time his front tires nearly went into the gutter by the curb and he had to wrench it back onto the road. This was an overcompensation that brought him swerving in front of a cab. The driver slapped his horn and waved his fist at Billy.

Billy just waved and mouthed, "Sorry," before turning the corner and racing off. He was only a few blocks from Saint Michael's and he spotted the tall church spire with the silver cross atop it. But he was really thinking of breasts, finally sculpted, round, grapefruit-sized female breasts.

Damn, he thought leaning down over his handlebars to get more speed. *I might have to go to confession after mass. Aw, hell.*

☗ ☗ ☗

Working as a cigarette girl at the Gray Owl Casino, Paula Wozcheski liked to sleep in late. She had seen very little of her boyfriend, Blackjack Bobby Crandall, the last few days…and nights. Mostly due to all the weird things that has been happening throughout the city recently.

Seated at her kitchen table, dressed in her worn pink bathrobe, Paula looked through the morning edition of the Cape Noire Tribune and her attention was focused on the main article by reporter Sally Paige. If anyone had their hands on the pulse of the city, it was Sally Paige. Paula puffed on a cigarette and wondered if Bobby had been involved with any of the stuff hinted at in the article. When she saw Brother Bones mentioned, a cold chill ran up her spine.

Paula set her smoke in a glass ashtray and took another sip of the black coffee she had poured herself before sitting down. To her right the mid-morning sun was lighting up the heavy green shade over the window. The java calmed her thoughts.

The grim masked Undead Avenger known as Brother Bones, had saved Paula's life months ago when her husband, Janos, a dock worker, had become the member of a heinous cult and actually tried to have her sacrificed to some unspeakable sea demon. At the last possible moment, Bones, accompanied by Bobby, had arrived to defeat the cultists and destroy the beast …or at least sent it back to whatever hell had spawned it.

In the intervening weeks Paula had managed to get her life back on track. It wasn't easy maintaining her apartment only only one paycheck, but she managed. And then Bobby had started coming on to her in a more than friendly way.

The freckle-faced, red-headed card dealer was cute and she found herself attracted to him. Enough so that she eventually agreed to a date. It ended in her bed, much to Paula's surprise. Still, Bobby proved to be a thoughtful lover as well as a friend. Even to the point of helping her with some of her bills and buying groceries every now and then.

"Hey, I eat here almost as much as you do," he'd chuckled when she first had protested. But in the end she had given in. Pride was one thing, foolish stubbornness another.

Bobby had never completely confided in her what his relationship was with the gruesome Brother Bones, but she soon learned the creepy vigilante lived with her beau and there was no chance he would be moving in with her any time soon.

Taking another drag from her now nearly finished cigarette, Paula started to turn the pages to the classified ads section. Maybe it was time to start looking for her own roommate. Bobby wouldn't like it, but what was she suppose to do?

As she flipped the pages, her eye spotted the photo of two different boxers on the sports page. She opened the newspaper wide to see it was a promotional piece advertising a heavy-weight boxing match for the championship to be held at the McCoy Sports Stadium in town. Local hero, Big Bear Anderson would be squaring off against some foreigner named Lazlo Varkaine. The black and white photo was out of focus and showed the bare-chested fighter as having a gaunt, dark complexion with a haughty look about him as he held up his gloved hands in a challenging pose.

She shrugged, losing interest immediately. From what little she'd read, Anderson would mop up the ring with this so called, "Buiser From Bavaria."

Sheesh, what will they come up with next?

Paula went back to scouting the classifieds.

The wail of the speeding ambulance cut through city's downtown district causing other vehicles to immediately pull out of the way. It's bubble-top light flashing, the white emergency vehicle zipped through crowded intersections and a few red lights until it came to a screeching halt in front of the headquarters building of radio station WXYZ.

The back doors popped open and out leapt the dapper radio personality, Preston Elliot, resplendent in a new blue suit and white cravat. He walked to the passenger door and there handed the orderly a fifty-dollar bill.

"There you go, Henry. As ever, thanks for the lift."

Henry grinned and waved the bill at the driver who nodded approvingly. "Thank you, Mr. Preston. Same time next week."

"Indeed, old chap. Take care and have a jolly day."

The ambulance pulled away from the sidewalk and the handsome actor started for the revolving doors.

"You know, you could get into a great deal of trouble with that stunt," a clear and vibrant female voice said from his right.

He turned to see his co-star, the gorgeous Flora Reynolds, approaching wearing the latest in fashion, a fox-fur wrapped around her shoulders and a cute little black beret on her head.

Elliot chuckled. "Flora, darling, you know how horrendous traffic is at this time of the day. A taxi would never get me here on time for the show."

"And so you hire an ambulance, how ingenious." She took his offered arm and together they pushed through the turning glass doors. "That's something Thomas Bonaparte would do, I'm sure."

"Exactly, my dear, just keeping in character." Both of them laughed merrily as they moved through the expansive front lobby.

The building itself housed a dozen different business with the radio station taking up the top three floors.

As the care-free duo made their way towards the bank of elevators along the back wall, Preston Elliot couldn't help but think how lucky they really were. No sooner had WXYZ, at his suggestion, launched the TenaciTea Mystery Hour featuring Cape Noire's legendary boogey man than the stark, skull-masked character had actually appeared to thwart as yet another disastrous threat to the great metropolis. He'd even brought the battle to this very building and the climatic end of the so-called Dragon, had begun atop their own roof.

Of course only Elliot and a handful of people knew the truth as the papers had claimed the next day that the station had been attacked by a group of anarchists intent on blowing it to smithereens. Brother Bones, according to the fabricated story, had then appeared and defeated them in a bloody gun battle.

Was it any wonder their audience had tripled overnight, lighting up the telephone boards and filling their mail with thousands of new, excited fans wanting more adventures of the so-called Undead Avenger, Brother Bones.

And all of it had been Preston Elliot's glorious idea. The talented thespian not only played the lead character, Thomas Bonaparte aka Brother Bones, on the weekly broadcast, but also wrote the scripts. If this success continued, he was going to have to ask Station Manager Bill Fraley for a raise.

He and Miss Reynolds had just reached the four elevators and were awaiting the next box when a tall, effete fellow sidled up to them holding a rolled up manuscript in his gloved hands and wearing a bowler.

"Greetings, Elliot, Flora, how are we doing this fine day?" Steve Traynor was a pompous ass who had somehow managed to sustain a career in acting despite his second-rate talent. Word around the station was that he was related to Fraley's wife, Edna; some sort of second cousin or some such and it was she who, taken by his bogus charm, had cajoled her husband into giving him a job.

Elliot had seen the tall, scarecrow-like actor in a small production of *The Merchant of Venice* years ago and had never forgotten how ridiculously bad he was. And still, despite his loud protestation, the stuffed, no-talent hack had been foisted on him.

"Oh, we're just dandy," Flora Reynolds musically replied amused at Elliot's obvious discomfort in being next to Traynor. "And you, Steve?"

"Well I've certainly been better, dear." He held up the script in front of Elliot's face. "I really don't understand how you came to cast me as Bonaparte's ignorant taxi driver stooge, Gus."

"Really?" Elliot was grateful when the chime rang announcing a car had arrived. "I just naturally assumed an actor of your range and experience would have been thrilled at the challenge of playing against type." He noticed the smirk on Reynold's face as the elevator doors opened and they started to step in.

"But what about the lawyer, Anthony Nolan? Certainly he's much more suited to my image and personality."

Preston Elliot stepped past Chuck, the young elevator operator, slipped a five spot and whispered, "Make it fast, kid, before I strangle him."

Flora Reynolds heard the exchange and had to put a gloved hand over her mouth before she broke out laughing. Instead she coughed.

"Are you alright?" the obtuse Traynor asked.

"Oh, yes. Just a new perfume, it tickles my nose."

Preston Elliot rolled his eyes as the elevator started up.

💀 💀 💀

Because all the station's shows were recorded before a studio audience, the elevator was located directly across from the open doors to the small stadium while the actual offices of the company's staff etc. were located to the right and left corridors.

As he came out of the elevator, Preston Elliot saw the clock over the stadium entrance read 2:30 p.m. They still had thirty minutes before the show went live. He, Miss Reynolds and the still chattering Steve Traynor marched into the hall which was now filling up with people; most of them out of town tourists anxious to see a real radio melodrama up close.

Most of the stage area was bare save for sound microphones on stands, their wires criss-crossing like mating snakes all leading to an enclosed booth to the left in which several sound technicians could be seen through the clear glass. One of these was the Chief Sound Engineer, Gary Carlson; a man of average height, tufts of gray hair over his ears and a bald top. Carlson was a perfectionist with a quick temper and as he checked the volume levels of each individual stage mic, he was chomping on a big black cigar, gray smoke curling up around his face. Carlson had been known to throw temper tantrums in the middle of a recording if any of his three assistants failed to perform their duties flawlessly. So the crew put up with his gruffness as all of them knew Carlson was the best in the business.

Several young teenage girls, upon spotting the trio walking to the side stairs, jumped up and began shoving pencils and notebooks at Elliot and Reynolds asking for autographs. That none of them gave Traynor a second look didn't fail to register with Elliot and out of the corner of his eye he watched his pompous colleague push past all of them in a huff, mumbling about having no time for such foolishness.

Having placated their happy fans, the actors started up the stairs to the stage where Dave Holliway was checking over his props on his table near the back curtains. Holliway was the foley operator tasked with creating the various sound effects used throughout the show to include everything from thunder and lighting, to gunshot sounds and feet sloshing through thick mud.

Reynolds, removing her wrap, noticed Traynor had disappeared behind the curtains; most likely gone to his private dressing room.

"You really should stop picking on poor Steven," she chided Elliot as she went to the clothes rack at the far right of the stage. "You're incorrigible."

"The man is a total ass," the dashing celebrity said in a low voice as to not be overhead by those people seated in the first row.

Just then, Polly Mathews, the script girl, appeared from behind the dark purple curtains carrying the day's final shooting scripts. It was her job, once they were all typed up, to deliver them to the cast on stage just prior to going on air. When she saw Elliot was present, she hurried over to him.

"Oh, I'm glad you're early," she told him handing over a copy of a slim manuscript in a green folder. "The boss wanted to see you the second you got here."

"Alright, Polly. Thanks."

Elliot dashed behind the back curtains into the large hallway and made his way to the last door adorned with a placard reading STATION MANAGER. He knocked, heard Bill Fraley's reply and opened the door.

He was surprised to see his boss had company. Seated in one of the two big stuffed chairs in front of Fraley's desk was one of the most beautiful women Preston Elliot had ever beheld. She had lustrous black hair, a classical shaped face, with full lips, high cheekbones and two piercing green eyes under delicately arched brows. She was dressed in a conservative gray outfit, her long lovely legs crossed, the skirt raised up to show them off and beneath her jacket a starched white blouse, with a black cameo choker around her neck.

Breath-taking was the only word that came to Elliot's mind upon seeing her. She, in turn, looked at him with a curious expression as if sizing him up before committing to even a small smile.

"Ah, there you are, Preston," the middle-aged, stout manager exclaimed pointing his hand at the new arrival. "I'd like you to meet Miss Alexis Wyld..."

Wyld? Wasn't that the name of the mobster who once ran the city before he was gunned down? Didn't he have a daughter...?

"...and her assistant, Mr. Garrett."

Elliot was half-way across the room when he noticed the man standing in the corner behind the seated woman. Then he wondered how he could have possibly missed seeing him. Wearing a custom-fitted chauffeurs' uniform, Mr. Garrett was a huge, powerful man with square shoulders and a brown face that appeared to have been cut out of shiny Italian marble. Hands folded over his chest, he looked more like a Michelangelo statue than a living being.

Assistant, my foot! Elliot knew a bodyguard when he saw one.

"How do you do, Miss Wyld," he greeted while holding her outstretched hand. He nodded to the big man, "Mr. Garret, my pleasure, I'm sure." Garrett tipped his head slightly acknowledging the greeting.

"Sit down, Preston," Fraley said, obviously excited, "sit down. Miss Wyld is here to assume the sponsorship of your show. Isn't that great news?"

Easing himself down in the second chair, Elliot's surprise was genuine. "Really? You are going to bankroll the TenaciTea Mystery Hour?"

"Well, my financial advisors suggested it would be good advertising since I recently purchased the Shiloh Bottling company." Alexis Wyld said matter-of-factly. "Since the death of its owner, Edgar Shiloh, the company had gone into receivership and I was able to acquire it for a very reasonable price."

"So, you are going into the tea-making business?"

Finally a tiny smirk appeared on Wyld's beautiful face. "Actually, we are converting the plant into a brewery. We hope to start making and distributing Wyld Ale throughout this region within the next few months."

"I see, then we'll have to get our marketing people to whip up some new copy to showcase your product."

"I will leave that in your capable hands, Mr. Elliot."

"Please, call me Preston. After all it seems you will now be paying my weekly stipend."

"That is correct…Elliot. And though I have no intentions of interfering with how you present your show, there are two things I feel I must insist upon if Wyld Ale is to be the new sponsor."

Now it was Fraley's turn to fidget. He tugged at his tight Arrow shirt collar. "Anything, Miss. Wyld, whatever you want changed, we'll be only too glad to accommodate you. Isn't that right, Preston?"

Elliot Preston cocked an eyebrow unsure what was coming next.

"Ah, please, gentlemen, relax," Alexis Wyld laughed softly. "I'm actually a big fan of your show and I sincerely do not wish to change it in any way."

"I see," Elliot responded. "And your two directives are?"

"What I just said for one, that you do not change the show's format. Again, I think your adventures of this Brother Bones are marvelous and wish for you to continue writing them just as you've been doing."

"Well…ah…thank you, Miss Wyld. I'm most flattered and delighted you enjoy the show so much. And your second request?"

"You have a standing offer of fifty-thousands dollars to anyone who can provide you with hard evidence on the existence and whereabouts of this Brother Bones. Is that correct?"

"Ahem, well, we did. But with Mr. Shiloh's passing and…"

"Elliot, I want you to increase the amount to fifty-five thousand."

"What?"

"You heard me. I will personally pay fifty-five thousand dollars to anyone who can provide me with verifiable information concerning Brother Bones and his current whereabouts."

Ten minutes later the elevator doors slipped open in the building's underground parking garage and Alexis Wyld stepped out followed by the towering Lucas Garrett.

As they walked across the huge subterranean enclosure heading for her expensive, silver colored Duesenberg, she sensed the big man's concerns.

"Something bothers you, Lucas?"

"I am puzzled as to why you would involve yourself with such frivolity, Miss Wyld."

"How do you mean?"

"Your one goal is to find Brother Bones and destroy him, and yet you …"

"Finance the radio program broadcasting his adventures."

"Exactly, madam. I fail to see the logic."

They reached the expensive automobile and as Garrett opened the rear door, Alexis looked up at him and elaborated. "My father taught me that the only way to destroy one's enemy is to know everything about them; their strengths and their weaknesses. For the most part, Bones is still an enigma, one I need to understand before I can take action."

"And you believe this radio show will aid you in the accumulation of such the knowledge?"

"Think of it, Lucas, thousands of people throughout the city listening in every week and knowing they could easily be fifty-five thousand dollars richer simply by looking out for our target."

"Therefore making them your unwitting accomplices in the hunt." Garrett bowed slightly before his mistress. "An ingenious strategy, madam."

"Thank you, Lucas. I thought you would approve. Now let's hurry and get home so that we don't miss today's show."

The bailiff stood up in the courtroom and bellowed, "All rise for the Honorable Judge Melvin Creston Williams."

Several dozen bodies rose off of hard wooden seats and watched as the black-robed Judge Williams of Cape Noire's Superior Court emerged from a side door, stepped up onto the raised dais behind the massive bench. There, he grabbed his worn, teakwood gavel.

He banged it loudly on the receiving block, looked over the parties at both the defendant's table and those at the state's and then said, "This court is now in session. Be seated, please."

Once she had sat down, reporter Sally Paige turned to ace photographer, John Finlay, who was putting a new flashbulb into his flash-pan, and whispered. "Make sure to get a shot of Lassiter after the sentence is handed down."

Finlay, a likeable, veteran newshound, leaned over and whispered back, "I know my job, Paige. Don't sweat it."

Meanwhile, His Honor the judge was getting things going. "Will the defendant, Darren Lassiter please stand."

At the defense table, an anxious, fearful young man stood up with his lawyer, a court appointed counselor, and looked up at Judge Williams.

"Darren Lassiter, last week you were found guilty of the crime of murder by a jury of your peers. It is now my duty to hand down your sentence. Do you have anything to say before I pass judgment on you?"

The condemned man shrugged and said, "Naw, why bother. It ain't gonna change nothing."

"Very well then," the gray haired judge continued. "You are hereby sentenced to death by electrocution one month from today at the state penitentiary. May God have mercy on your soul."

Williams rapped his gavel again at the same time John Finlay and several other photographers in the room snapped their pictures, light flashes popping over the judge's final words. "The matter before this court is concluded."

Paige scribbled a few sentences hastily in her notebook as two police officers escorted Darren Lassiter out of the court via a side door.

Rushing out into the cavernous corridors outside the room, Paige was all set to return to the Tribune with Finlay when she saw the Chief of Detectives, Lt. Dan Rains, talking to a thin man in an outdated suit outside the District Attorney's office.

"Head on back without me," she told her colleague. "Tell Anderson I'll be back after lunch and get the story written up in plenty of time."

"Alright," Finlay said moving away. "But it's your neck if you don't. You know the chief."

"I'll be there. Now get that photo developed...pronto."

As soon as Finlay had disappeared down the curved stairway to the ground floor, the brunette reporter returned her attention to the cop and the little man.

They were shaking hands as she approached them and heard the end of Lt. Rains' comments. "...doing the right thing, Mr. Wilkens. Trust me."

"Well I hope you're right." With that the man put on his hat and walked off. Rains looked up and saw Paige.

"So, what's the Cape Noire Tribune's number one crime reporter doing here today?" he grinned.

"Just covering the Lassiter sentencing," she answered nodding her head back towards the now empty courtroom.

"How'd it go?"

"Williams gave him the chair. A month from today."

"Hmm, no surprise there," the police bull commented, pushing his fedora back on his head. "It's just too bad it's the kid we nabbed and not his old man, Deke."

"Hey, you'll get him, I've all the faith in the world in you, Rains."

"Ha, now that's a surprise. Usually your stories depict me and my men as no better than Keystone Cops."

"Whatever sells papers, Rains. Speaking of such, who was the little dude you were just talking to?'

"None of your business, Sally. Just forget about it."

"Only if you'll buy a working girl lunch?"

The good-looking Rains smiled. "Okay, how about Lou's Diner across the street. I hear the blue plate special today is fried chicken."

"Oh, Lieutenant, you do know how to treat a lady lavishly."

"That I do, Sally. But you're no lady."

At that she took his arm and started leading him towards the stairs. "How true, how true."

The tarot cards were all laid out before Countess Selena and she studied them carefully.

"The good, the evil, and the poor innocent souls all caught up in these intersecting lines like the threads in a bloody tapestry."

There was no one else in the room with her, but the seer sensed the spirits of those that had gone on surrounding her—comforting her—and so she often spoke aloud.

"And the dead man who walks, Brother Bones, will be at the center of all this ju-ju and his guns will speak and the battle will go on.

"The Dragon is gone, but for Brother Bones there is no rest.

"No rest at all."

THE BUTCHER'S FESTIVAL

The Sixth Street bus arrived with a belch of exhaust fumes, and the four people huddled under the corner depot roof did their best to stay out of the rain. Heavy winds coming off the bay were sending the fat raindrops sideways, and there was little protection in the flimsy tin shack. The quartet, consisting of an old man, a heavy-set woman, a hotel maid and a thin, nervous fellow, lined up along the vehicle's dented yellow side as the driver opened the door and disgorged several passengers.

One of the exiting citizens was a short fellow with thick glasses who looked around nervously upon stepping onto the slick sidewalk.

The four waiting passengers hurried aboard and shuffled down the aisle of the nearly full bus to find an empty seat. The thin man, named Irving Wilkens, spotted an empty seat at the rear and made for it as the driver shifted into gear and stepped on the gas.

Dropping into the seat, he looked over and eyed a small package crudely wrapped with brown butcher's paper. He started to reach for it when it blew up.

Outside, back at the at the bus stop, the small man with the glasses watched the big bus explode with a powerful boom, its frame leaping off the road before dissolving into millions of tiny pieces, among them steel, rubber and human tissue and bone.

The little man took off his glasses, wiped them with a handkerchief and strolled off into the rain, a dark, sadistic smile on his face. He loved blowing things up.

☠ ☠ ☠

Less than an hour later, in a dingy, darkened room a figure stirs in the worn upholstered chair facing a rain-washed window. Night is descending quickly and with it the shadows that invade his tiny, square domain. On the bureau to the left of the window a single candle suddenly sputters to life, its solitary flame casting an eerie glow. The dweller rises from his seat and approaches the fire as a face begins to materialize in the flickering

17

orange fingers. It is of a long-dead girl, robbed of her life by a sadistic, soulless gunman—one who now does her bidding.

"Violence and death have come once more," she utters in a sweet, lilting voice. The thing standing before her merely listens, acknowledging her words only by his grave-like silence. "You are needed once more. Justice will be meted out by your hands."

The undead avenger nods as he reaches for a milk-white porcelain mask laying next to the dancing candle. Brother Bones affixes the skull-like visage to the horror that is his true face, his dark eyes blinking through the twin holes.

"Where?"

☠ ☠ ☠

Standing in front of the big warehouse steel door under the single overhead light bulb, Cody Randall reflected for the hundredth time on how much she despised Cape Noire. All around her was nothing but a stygian blackness and a damp, cold breeze left over from the day's downpour. At least it wasn't raining now, which was a small consolation to be grateful for. Still, here she was, decked out in her cowboy jeans, hat and black felt domino mask standing in front of a massive door about to once again battle the forces of evil.

Damn, but a smart girl could find a much nicer, safer career, the lovely lass known as the Pulptress mused as she thumped the door for the third time in as many minutes with the stock of her pump-action shotgun.

There was a click from behind the door and the small, rectangular peep shutter slipped open to reveal a pair of beady eyes under heavy thick eyebrows.

"Yeah, yeah, whataya want?" the dimwitted gangster asked, looking down at the strangely garbed female standing on the landing.

"I want to see your boss, Pete Malone."

"What for?"

"Well, that's really between me and him now, but then again, you really are in for a world of shit."

"Huh?"

Cody tilted her cowboy hat back, stepped closer to the peep slot and whispered, "Listen, moron, there's a dozen ninjas coming down on this place even as we speak. Now I think that's something your boss would like to know. Don't you?"

The big guard kept staring at her and she wondered just how stupid he really was. Then there was a chunking noise and he was gone from sight just before the big door opened inwards.

He was standing there with one hand out. "Okay, Calamity Jane, hand over the shotgun and the six-iron and I'll take you to see the boss."

Cody could have blown a hole through him easily enough, and the temptation was great. Still, those ninjas we're not going to sit around waiting to make their move, and if they killed Malone before she got to him, then her plan would go down the drain in a quick flush.

She passed over the shotgun and then the Colt six-shooter from its holster riding low on her right hip. "Alright, you satisfied now?"

"Come on. Down the corridor there and stay in front of me."

Cody complied with his orders and started down the dimly illuminated aisle as the brutish thug slammed the door shut again and slipped the steel bolt in place.

There were steel shelves to either side filled with various crates containing all kinds of manufacturing supplies. Cody had done her homework and knew the business itself was a legitimate front used by Malone to clean the money he earned from his more nefarious enterprises. Cape Noire was still an open city as far as its underworld inhabitants were concerned, ever since the Boss of Bosses, Topper Wyld, had been wasted by the white faced grim reaper known as Brother Bones. Malone was one of the smaller sharks vying for a bigger piece of the criminal pie.

Cody recognized him from the various newspaper mug shots, as he sat at the back of the building, laid out with three desks, steel cabinets and other assorted business paraphernalia; all bathed under three low hanging florescent tubes. The area was dead center of the main floor and Malone, seated in front of a long table covered with bricks of cocaine, was surrounded by half a dozen men all cut from the same Neantherdal mold, each heavily armed and dangerous.

Peter Tomlin Malone was an average looking fellow with thinning gray hair, a neat mustache and thick eye-glasses. Cody thought he looked more like an accountant than a mobster and she noted the predominant eye-glasses were similar to those worn by his brother Arnold; the reason for her visit.

Now Malone was adjusting those glasses, as he looked up at her and the towering guard who had escorted her to his inner sanctum.

"So, Otto, who the hell do we have here?"

"Don't know, boss. She said she had to talk to you and that there were nin...nin..."

"The actual word is ninja-jitsu," Cody provided, wanting to get on with her purpose. She could sense the shadow warriors were only minutes from launching their assaults.

"Ninjas?" Malone sat back in his stiff back chair, now studying the lithe young woman in the western get-up and mask. "Lady, just who the hell are you and what do you want here?"

"My name is Cody Randall. I'm a bounty hunter."

"Big deal, last I looked there were no outstanding warrants with my name on them."

"I'm not here for you. It's your brother I want."

"Arnie? You're after my little brother. Lady, you got a real set of balls, you know that?"

"I also know there are six ninjas overhead about to cut loose. I'd guess a rival gang is after your turf."

"That's the biggest whopper I've heard yet," Malone scoffed. "Otto, show her the door and make sure she don't come back."

"Sure thing, bo—" Otto's reply ended in mid-phrase as a whistling noise came out of nowhere and ended with a loud smack as a steel star suddenly appeared in the middle of his forehead. Blood began to seep out as his eyes dulled, trying to see the offending instrument of his demise, then he started falling forward.

Cody spun around and pulled the shotgun out of his hand just as another whistle pierced the air. She instinctively whipped the barrel up to her face and it deflected the second shuriken sending it ricocheting off to her right.

Meanwhile a dead Otto crashed into Malone's sorting table, topping stacks of drugs as several other spinning missiles rained down from the rafters above.

All hell broke loose.

Cody pumped a shell with one jerk of her hand, then fired upward just as a black-clad assassin appeared above her. The shotgun blast caught him in the chest and propelled him backward.

Meanwhile Malone's goons were dancing back and forth; guns pointed every which way trying to find a target. While the black-clad assassins seemed to emerge out of the surrounding shadows, strike and then vanish in the blink of an eye. Within thirty seconds half of the gunmen were down from either throwing stars or sword cuts.

Cody had dropped to one knee, using the table as cover while she dug her Colt Peacemaker out from under Otto's dead body.

Two ninjas landed like cats on the table just as Malone fell backwards out of his chair, the only thing that saved his life as a razor-sharp katana blade clove the air where his head had been. Still, he had the presence of mind to open up with his own .38 caliber handgun as he toppled over, three shots catching the first ninja in the chest. The second rose up in a crouch, blade ready when the table top ruptured upward from the shotgun load and tore away his genitals and belly in a spray of blood. He died screaming.

The Pulptress sprung up from her kneeling position and fired another blast towards the ceiling second before a steel chain suddenly wrapped itself around the barrel's tip. Her eyes widened as the weapon was ripped out of her hands and vanished into the darkness.

Damn! She whipped out the Colt and backed up into a mobster with half his head sliced off. He made a gurgling sound in his throat before collapsing in front of her.

This wasn't going exactly as planned, and with most of Malone's goons dropping like flies, the outcome for her continued well being was diminishing rapidly.

Suddenly, three of the wraithlike, silent warriors dropped to the floor surrounding her, katana blades aimed at her. Cody fanned her pistol and the masked killer to her front lost the top of his head. At least she'd go down fighting, she thought, ready to feel cold steel ripping through her back.

Instead, there came the booming of two loud shots and both ninjas were thrown off their feet, gaping wounds in their chests. Cody spun about to see another fighter enter the fray unlike any other she had ever seen before. Tall, draped in a worn, black overcoat and wearing a beat up slouch hat, the shooter marched into the kill zone with twin silver plated .45 automatics blasting away, his targets both the ninjas and Malone's thugs. And as he came into the harsh, cold light of the florescent lamps, she saw his bone white porcelain mask just before he began to laugh.

Brother Bones!

His guns continued to boom as he approached her, a sulfur stench permeateing the air around him. He was the creepiest thing she had ever seen, which was saying a great deal.

Suddenly, he stiffened as two feet of hard steel ruptured out of his chest, impaling him. Bones looked down at the sword sticking out of his chest and merely shook his head, the small assassin behind him still holding on to the leather handle, as another ninja suddenly sprung up in front of the undead avenger.

Bones, still clutching his guns, blew away the new threat and then twisted around hard, tearing the blade out of its wielder's grasp. Then, before the small oriental killer realized what was happening, Brother Bones reached down and embraced him, driving the sword that had penetrated his own carcass into the silent killer, bonding them together. The ninja tried to scream only to have his lungs fill with blood which then spewed out of his mouth as he died, going limp in the avenger's arms.

"Have you seen enough?" Bones asked the Pulptress as he opened his arms and the dead ninja slid off the now blood-soaked katana and crumbled at his feet.

Cody looked around her, the area had become a slaughter house with bodies strewn everywhere. Then she saw Pete Malone stumbling away into the back of the building to lose himself from the copious bloodletting. Without a second thought, she put one hand on the money table and vaulted over it to give chase.

"Stop!" Brother Bones called out but she ignored him. Without Malone she would be never find his brother, the Butcher.

The frightened Malone had disappeared around a corner which led to another hallway. Turning into it, Cody froze as she was instantly enveloped in a thick, cloying darkness. Somewhere ahead there was a scraping noise along the floor, something heavy being moved.

Frantically, she dug into her jeans pockets and produced a wooden match which she lit with a flick of her index fingernail. Ahead of her was a narrow hallway she could just barely make out. She started off cautiously, her gun cocked and ready to shoot should Malone be hiding in ambush.

An old, worn rug covered part of the floor, and as she put her foot down on it the entire fabric caved inward and she fell through the hidden aperture. Cody had been trained to react far quicker than normal people, and the second she began to fall, she tossed her pistol and the match, both hands frantically clawing for a grip anywhere.

They caught the edge of square cut out, stopping her descent as rug continued to fall until she heard a soft splash. She dangled over the open sewer unable to see anything within the dark recesses beneath her. She could faintly hear someone moving further away, sloshing through the water.

Before she could decide what to do next, a big hand wrapped itself around her right wrist and she was pulled upward like a prize fish and set on the floor again. In the inky world around her, she could just barely discern Brother Bones shape.

"Thanks," she gasped, reaching into her jeans to find another match.

"I told you to stop."

She scratched the sulfur tip to find him standing right in front of here, the light shining off that smooth ivory colored mask. Cody stifled a scream, aware of how silent Bones moved, much like the wraith he appeared to be.

"Give me a heart attack, why don't you?" she barked, trying to get her nerves calm. "Just what the hell are you doing here, Bones?"

"I am here to help you…"

"Mission accomplished."

"…find Arnold Malone."

"The Butcher. Why?"

"I will explain later. Come, our prey has eluded us." With that he moved down the empty corridor leaving Cody behind to pick up her gun just as the expiring match burned her fingers.

"Ouch."

Brother Bones moved around the trap door and she stayed close behind him.

"You knew that was there, didn't you?"

"Yes, there are hundreds of these under the streets of Cape Noire. They saw much use during the days of prohibition."

Cody smelled brine. "Is that the sea I smell?"

"Yes. The tunnel leads to Malone's dockside hideout. We will get there much quicker by car."

"Lead the way."

A few minutes later they were back in the warehouse proper, moving past the dead bodies.

"Bones, hold up a second."

The grim bringer of death halted as Cody came up around him and tapped the katana blade still sticking out of his chest. He looked down surprised to see it was still there.

"Remove it, please."

Cody stepped around him, the brimstone stench on him pervasive. Using both hands, she clasped the sword handle and pulled the Japanese short sword from his body. Brother Bones grunted and continued his exit out of the building.

☗ ☗ ☗

"REMOVE IT, PLEASE."

Cody Randall also retrieved her shotgun by the time she and Brother Bones left the warehouse and started across the slick, empty parking lot. Thunder rolled somewhere off in the far distance and she searched the clouded skies, hoping whatever foul weather was on its way would hold off a while longer.

"Where the hell are we going?" she said to Bones' back.

Her answer came wheeling out of a nearby alley in the shape of an old, dented-up gray roadster that pulled up in front of them with a squeal of the brakes.

"Get in the front," Bones commanded as he opened the rear door. She complied, holding her hat with one hand and shotgun in the other as she fell back into the seat beside the driver; a freckle-faced, red-headed kid with a goofy smile on his face.

"Hi, I'm Bobby Crandall, my friends call me Blackjack."

"Really?"

"I'm a card dealer at the Gray Owl casino."

"Well, ah…nice to meet you. I'm Cody Randall."

"I know," a nod to the figure in the backseat. "He told me."

"Drive, Crandall," Brother Bones interrupted. "Malone has fled to his hideout on Pier Sixteen. We will find him and his brother there."

"Gotcha, Boss." Crandall shifted into gear and stomped on the gas pedal sending the roadster speeding off into the deserted streets of Cape Noire.

Okay, thought Cody, *it's catch up time.*

"So one of you want to fill me on what's going on here?"

"Sure," Crandall agreed as he pulled them around a sharp corner never once letting up on the accelerator. "What do you want to know, Miss Randall?"

Miss Randall? Geez, was this kid real? Then again, he was cute.

"Well for starters, just call me Cody, okay? And how the hell do you and Bones here know so damn much about my business in Cape Noire?"

"The Boss has a spirit guide."

"A what?"

"The soul of a young girl who appears to him every so often when innocent lives have been taken. Which is what happened two days ago."

Crandall went on to explain that a local crusading attorney had convinced one of Pete Malone's accountants to turn state evidence against him for a fat financial reward. Somehow, Malone had gotten wind of the betrayal and dispatched his psycho sibling, Arnold, to take care of the problem. Arnold Malone, known as the Butcher, did so by blowing up the downtown bus on which the accountant traveled daily. In the process he also killed thirteen innocent passengers.

"Their souls cry out for vengeance," Brother Bones added at the end of Crandall's tale. "My spirit guide sent me to avenge them. She also told me another seeker of truth and justice had come to Cape Noire and I was to find and save her."

"Meaning me? Your spirit guide told you about me?"

"Yes."

"Don't you find that a little strange?" Cody looked back at the undead creature with the porcelain mask, and realized she had just asked a dead man if he thought ghosts were strange. "Right. Forget I asked."

Crandall chuckled, "He does take some getting use to."

"No fooling." They were leaving the main boulevards for narrower streets. She could make out wharves and anchored ships through the gaps between the old buildings they were passing.

"So tell me, Blackjack, how'd you get hooked up in all this?"

Crandall eased up on the gas pedal as they rolled onto the road skirting the piers. A dense fog was beginning to slide in from the bay. His headlights barely penetrated the thick blanket of condensation.

"Two years ago he saved me from being shot by his twin brother."

"His brother?"

"It's a long story. Anyway I owe him and the work he does means something. So I help in whatever way I can."

Crandall slowed the roadster to a crawl, peered at a dilapidated building front and then stopped the car. "We're here."

☻ ☻ ☻

Cody Randall clutched her shotgun to her bosom, standing beside the Undead Avenger as they looked up at the words, Hanson Boat Builders. Faded letters on a crooked sign over the main doors to the wooden structure.

"Stay with me," his gravelly voice ordered. "Do what I say without hesitation."

"I'm not use to taking orders," she said matter-of-factly.

"Then stay with Crandall in the car."

She pulled her cowboy hat down and glared at him, her show of bravado lost on his stoic demeanor.

Didn't anything ever get to this guy? "Alright, Bones, have it your way.

But let's hurry it up. I don't want them escaping us a second time."

Brother Bones seemed to nod, then he walked over to the iron padlock that wrapped around the twin door handles. Smoothly he produced his powerful .45 automatics and proceeded to blow the lock into small pieces. *BLAM! BLAM! BLAM!*

Cody moved past him, pulled off a loose section of chain and pulled the right half open by a few feet. "So much for the element of surprise, heh?"

"They knew we were coming," was all Bones would say as he moved past her into the shop's interior.

Unlike the business district warehouse, the boat shop was brightly lit from high hanging light bulbs and as they moved through it, Cody gave the place a careful visual inspection. A thick layer of sawdust covered the floor almost muting their footsteps as they moved around work benches, saw horses and various machines such as drills and lathes, all used in the manufacture of seaworthy crafts.

They passed all styles of boats from canoes to larger sailing ships, all assembled with different planks of lumber and steel spines for reinforcement. Several completed hulls were suspended upside down on pulleys from the ceiling, where they had been hoisted to allow coats of paint to dry properly. That was another thing Cody became aware of, the strong odors that saturated the shop from linseed oils to paint and alcohol based thinners. It was clear, despite its owner's nefarious illegal activities; Hanson Boat Builders was a genuine enterprise with lots of contracts.

"Hold it right there, Spook!" Pete Malone came out from behind a stack of old lobster crates with a Thompson submachine gun in his hands. Behind him emerged his brother, Arnold. He appeared unarmed, wearing a simple gray suit and black tie. Cody could see the family resemblance accentuated by the thick glasses both brothers wore.

"Your reckoning is upon you, Arnold Malone," Brother Bones announced, his own gleaming pistols pointing at the two Malone brothers.

"Is that a fact?" the small man retorted as he began unbuttoning his jacket. "Well, let's see how much you are willing to pay for this dance, Brother Bones."

With a flourish, Butcher Malone pulled opened his suit to reveal a strange corset of glass tubes that was wrapped around his middle.

"Dear God in heaven," Cody gasped. "What the hell is that stuff?"

"It's nitroglycerin, my dear. And the slightest bump to any of these vials could set it off...and then ...KABOOM! We're all history."

"So we have us a Mexican stand off," Pete Malone declared. "I suggest the two of you slowly turn around and walk out of here."

"That is not going to happen," Bones started to bring his right hand up, sighting along the top of his pistol. "Instead both of you are going to die here."

Cody sidled up to the black clad zombie warrior and whispered, "What are you doing? If that nitro goes, we're dead ducks. At least I am."

"No more talk, Pulptress. Shoot the Butcher."

"What? Are you crazy..."

Brother Bones squeezed the trigger and shot Pete Malone between the eyes. The mob boss's head rocked back, surprise in his eyes as his brain was demolished by the hot missile passing through it.

"NOOOO!!" Arnold Malone screamed, his hands reaching out to catch his falling brother.

Cody flipped the shotgun to her shoulder and fired. At the same time, Brother Bones aimed his pistols to the ceiling and unleashed another volley aiming at the steel chains overhead.

The shotgun blast ripped through the Butcher and nitro. The explosion erupted as a singular bright flare of white, sucking up all the noise in the area...then to Cody's utter shock, Bones was knocking her down just as the suspended rowboat that had been dangling over their heads came crashing down on them.

The bomb concussion slammed into the hull, tearing it to shreds, while beneath it Bones was huddled over the Pulptress. Then, within seconds of the blast there was a loud whooshing noise and flames sprang up throughout the building.

Brother Bones tossed aside the overturned, demolished husk and pulled Cody to her feet. They were surrounded by a fiery inferno as cans of thinner and paint went up like delayed bombs.

"Stay behind me and keep your mouth covered," Bones advised and then took off at a run for the front entrance. Cody hustled after him, the flames of the rapidly expanding blaze reaching after her like living fingers from hell.

Then they were both bursting free, into the cool, saving embrace of the night air. Back on the street, they continued to run until they had reached the roadster where Blackjack Crandall was standing, his face a visage of concern.

"Holy shit, what happened in there?" he asked, clearly relieved to have them back safe.

"A monster of unparalleled cruelty became his own final victim." Borther Bones put away his automatics, watching the old building be consumed in the roaring fire.

In the distance fire alarms were sounding.

"I think it's time we left," he said looking at Cody. "Will you accompany us?"

"No thanks, with Malone's death, my job here is done."

"Can we drop you off somewhere?" Bobby Crandall offered, hoping to spend a few more minutes with the sexy vigilante.

"Thanks, but I'm in the mood for a long walk."

"Suit yourself, Pulptress." Bones touched the tip of his slouch hat with a nod. "Till we meet again. Come along, Crandall, my work here is done."

The roadster was speeding away ten seconds later leaving Cody Randall, one of the Pulptress' many identities, behind, her shotgun resting across her shoulder. As soon as they were out of sight, she turned and started strolling towards the nearest alley. She didn't want to be anywhere near the place when the fire trucks arrived.

In the end, she'd failed to get her man, but then again, justice had triumphed in the form of the grim Brother Bones. Sometimes that had to be enough.

She whistled as she melted into the night.

THE END

THE BRUISER FROM BAVARIA

Mad Max Mulligan drove his massive right cross into Jake the Snake Arranta's jaw with a cannon-like blow. The scar-faced Arranta rocked back on his heels and saw stars. They were bright and shiny and spinning all around his rugged, prize-fighter's mug.

By now, the referee had moved in to keep a careful, professional eye on the two middle-weights as they slugged it out in this, the last of a three round preliminary bout. Clearly it appeared that the kid from the south end, Maxwell Arthur Mulligan at birth, was about to win his first major fight.

Wham! Wham! He kept driving his gloved fists into the Arranta's puss, keeping those stars spinning. The veteran boxer was clearly in a stupor and moving steadily backwards until the ropes brought him up short.

All around them, the paying customers roared their blood-lust, screaming as if in one booming voice for the blonde-haired, good-looking kid to finish off his battered opponent. Twenty-thousand modern day Romans all packed tightly in the McCoy Sports Arena. Not an empty seat in the house, and all screaming for blood. Lots of it.

Mulligan kept pounding away at the wreck that had been Arranta's ugly puss, when the ref slid between them and did his best to pull the kid off what he believed to be his helpless victim. The crowd, through the haze of cigarette and cigar smoke booed loudly, afraid they were about to be cheated of their pound of flesh.

"Let'em fight!" screamed an old woman seated directly behind Blackjack Bobby Crandall, instantly deafening his left ear.

"Geezuz!" Crandall cried, slapping his hand over his wounded ear. The old woman, dressed in a ratty shawl and smelling of castor oil, ignored him as she continued to harangue the referee with the rest of the throng.

How on earth anyone could enjoy this barbarism and call it sport was beyond the young, freckle-faced, red-headed card dealer. He found it hard to believe this was how he was spending his one night off from the Gray

Owl Casino. But all he had to do was look at the beautiful brunette seated to his right and his irritation melted away.

The recently widowed Paula Wozcheski did double-duty at the gambling establishment as both a cigarette and hat-check girl. She was a stunning, clear-eyed young woman with raven-colored hair and a figure to stop traffic. The first time Crandall had seen her in the club's traditional fishnet stockings and tight bustier top, he'd swallowed the gum he'd been chewing. He had also been disappointed to learn she was married to a brutish dock worker at the time.

Several months later, in a strange series of horrific events, her husband had died and Paula would have been sacrificed to some unspeakable monster from another dimension if not for the intervention of Crandall's master, the grim bone-faced avenger known as Brother Bones. Of course Paula had no idea it was Crandall who had brought Brother Bones into the matter thus ultimately rescuing her from death. She knew they were connected but had the good sense not to pry any further into the matter. In the months since the affair, she and the card dealer's friendship had evolved into a burgeoning romance.

Thus when he had suggested going out a few days earlier, it was Paula who had requested they attend the fights. It seemed she was a big fan, something she had inherited from her father back in Cleveland.

And here he sat, watching two grown men pound the hell out of each other solely in hopes of getting lucky. What a guy won't do for a little loving, he thought wryly. Still, Paula was gorgeous and putting up with a few hours of boxing was a small price to pay for that bit of heaven.

Crandall was so caught up in his own thoughts he failed to notice the match had ended until he heard the caterwauling boos from the crowd. Sure enough, the ref had put and end to Arranta's woes by pulling Mulligan off and ending the beating.

The winner made his obligatory dance around the ring before his handlers threw a robe around his shoulders and hustled him away. At the same time, the loser's team was exiting up another aisle.

Giving his fight card a quick look, Crandall was delighted to see the main event was next; meaning he only had to suffer through one more contest. The pamphlet listed the next pair of fighters as one Big Bear Anderson; a hometown boy and his opponent; Lazlo Vakraine known as the Bruiser From Bavaria.

"Hmm, a foreign dude," he mumbled to himself.

Paula heard him and leaning over offered, "Look at his records. He's twelve and O."

"Meaning?"

"Since turning pro, he's never lost a fight."

"Really. Then this should be good." Even though he was bored silly, the last thing Crandall wanted to do was allow Paula to think he wasn't having fun.

Then, the ring announcer, dressed in a fancy tuxedo, took the center ring, grabbed hold of the descending microphone and went into his boisterous spiel. "Ladies and gentlemen, we now come to this evening's main event; a thirteen round contest between two up and coming fighters, both vying for a shot at the heavyweight title.

"In the corner to my left, weighing in at one hundred and eighty-five pounds and hailing from right here in Cape Noire, our own Jake Big Bear Anderson!" The announcer pointed to his immediate left and a spotlight appeared over the contestant as he made his way to the ring followed by his entourage.

Crandall strained his head around Paula to get a better view of the big, tall black warrior in the blue robes. Anderson looked like a giant, his chiseled features and bald head gave off an aura of primal might as he marched past the cheering throngs. Here was a man ready to take on the world without the slightest thought of failure. He climbed into the ring, threw off his robe and revealed his powerful physique, raising his gloved hands high over his head for all to see. Crandall was reminded of the old fable of the steel driving man, John Henry, as the man seemed a flesh and blood personification of that legendary American hero.

He wondered what kind of man would be foolish enough to challenge Anderson. He didn't have long to wait for an answer as the flamboyant announcer once more sent his voice booming through the stadium speakers. "His opponent, weighing in at one hundred and seventy-six pounds, from overseas, with a record of twelve victories, eight by knock outs, and no losses, make way for Lazlo Vakraine, the Bruiser from Bavaria!"

A second group of men came marching down the aisle into the stadium, surrounding a tall, dark-haired boxer in a deep ruby red robe. As the group neared the end of the carpeted aisle, Blackjack was able to get a better look at Vakraine and what he saw startled him.

Lazlo Vakraine, although as tall as Anderson, was the complete opposite in physical appearances. His features were sharply edged, from a Roman like nose to a pointed chin and black eye brows that arched over penetrating eyes that reminded Crandall of an eagle. Yet what was most surprising was the color of his skin, or better yet the lack of coloring.

Stepping through the ropes, held open by his aids, the foreigner stood and allowed his trainer to remove his gaudy red robe to reveal his almost pure white body.

For a second Crandall thought the man might be an albino, but that wasn't the case. There was some pigmentation to Vakraine's skin, but it was of a sickly pallor. And yet the man's physique was trim and fit in all the right places. That these elements were contradictory puzzled the young man and he found himself sitting up straight in anticipation of what would happen when the bell sounded.

"Is it just me," he said to Paula, "or does that guy look like death warmed over?"

"Well, he is different looking than most boxers I've seen."

"That's an understatement. He looks like he could break if Anderson just taps him hard."

"Don't count on it, Bobby," the brunette argued. "Boxing is more than just guys pounding on each other. I've seen some pretty skillful fighters with less meat than him hold their own."

"Really?" Crandall appreciated Paula's superior knowledge on the subject, but he still had his doubts.

The referee had finished his talk with the two contestants, they slapped gloves and returned to their corners to await the bell. Anderson danced from foot to the other, seeming unable to contain the nervous energy that filled him, while the quiet Bavarian merely stood waiting, his hands down by his side as if he didn't have a care in the world.

The bell rang.

Big Bear charged across the canvas like a maddened bull and began swinging for all he was worth. The Bavarian barely had time to throw up his arms to ward off the blows. Still some connected with his shoulders and several bounced off his face to either side. The assaulted boxer fell back into his corner and tried to become a turtle, pulling his head down to avoid any more punches.

When the referee saw the fight wasn't progressing, he stepped in and pushed Anderson away, telling Vakraine to start fighting. The gaunt fighter nodded and hastily moved out of the corner and began circling the ring.

Slapping his gloves together in frustration, Big Bear snorted and came on again. This time Vakraine dodged his two blows and moving around the big man's left side, threw a punch into his ribs before dancing away. Annoyed, Anderson spun around and tried to stop his retreat, hoping to push him back against the ropes.

Then Big Bear threw a short jab with his right and then followed it with a lightning fast uppercut with the left that caught his opponent to the side of the head and rocked him. The crowd could sense Anderson's fury and was cheering for him to continue his attack, which he did.

Somehow Lazlo Vakraine managed to keep his feet beneath him, though it was clear he was wobbly as he kept moving backwards feebly warding off the black man's hammering blows. Yet somehow, as in the first round, despite the punishment he was taking, the pale foreigner managed to stay on his feet till the bell.

The next two rounds were similar, with Big Bear wailing on Vakraine and the Bavarian waltzing around him like a mobile punching bag. Blackjack Bobby Crandall was stymied, much like everyone else in the house, as to how the European boxer managed to endure the savage beating he was subjected to.

At the same time the majority of the crowd started to get restless, annoyed that they were witnessing such a lopsided fight and the boos and catcalls started up.

Then the fifth round began and a subtle change began to happen. Anderson's blows seemed to be slowing up and he was missing more times than connecting. Crandall thought the guy had most likely exhausted his strength in the early rounds and his tank was started to hit empty.

At the same time, Vakraine seemed more animated and began going on the offense, matching his foe punch for punch, some of which hit true. But the end of the round the crowd had stopped their foul cries sensing the shift that was happening.

"See, I told you so," Paula smirked, bending her lovely face to Blackjack. "He's really a wily boxer. Watch what happens now."

Crandall didn't require any inducements as by then he was totally into the pugilistic contest. Round six saw Vakraine coming to life for the very first time, as if his body was an old battery being recharged. His foot work was faster and he danced around Anderson like a gladiatorial ballet dancer, all the while striking at him with ever increasing blows that broke through the black man's defenses. The young card dealer was mesmerized. Vakraine's body seemed to be physically morphing before his eyes, the pallor taking on an odd sheen and the look on his face was one of cold, calculating fury.

Whereas Anderson had turned into a stumbling, weak combatant barely able to bring up his gloves, his face becoming drawn and haggard. *Geezus, what the hell is happening here?* Crandall thought to himself. *It's as if the stronger Vakraine gets, the weaker Anderson becomes.*

It was such a crazy thought, Crandall put it aside. Still, no matter the explanation, the tide had changed dramatically for Big Bear Anderson. He barely managed to make it through the sixth round. His trainer was frantic, as he collapsed on the small wooden stool in his corner. He and the others in Anderson's team were visibly shaken and doing their best to revitalize him before it was too late.

The bell rang for the seventh round and by a herculean effort, Big Bear stood up and began moving forward. He had a lost look on his face. Then Lazlo Vakraine fell on him like a starving wolf, raining down punches without let up until after a few seconds, the big American's eyes rolled up, showing their whites as he toppled over onto his back.

Like one massive organism, twenty thousand spectators rose to their feet and roared their approval. Meanwhile, leaning over the comatose fighter, the ref swung his right arm up and down like a pendulum, giving the mandatory ten count. The crowd picked up the chant loudly, their voices shaking the rafters.

"...SIX...SEVEN...EIGHT...NINE...TEN!"

The referee mouthed the words, "You're out!" but no one within ten feet could hear, so loud was the cheering in the stadium.

Lazlo Vakraine allowed the ref to take his right hand and hold it up, as his people climbed through the ropes and surrounded them, one holding up his hooded bathrobe.

At the same, Anderson's manager was on one knee trying to revive his boxer but his efforts were futile. Bending down to put his ear to the Big Bear's chest, the worried man was becoming frantic. Raising his head, he signaled the referee and mouthed the words, "Get the doc!"

McCoy's was Cape Noire's first rate sporting arena and maintained a ring doctor on staff during every venue. He was a middle aged fellow with brown hair and horn-rimmed glasses. As the word reached him via the ref, the grabbed his black medical bag and made his way into the ring, pushing through Vakraine's group and rushing to the injured Anderson.

He lifted Anderson's eye lids, then holding up his right hand, tried to feel for a pulse.

As expected, most of the people in the stadium were ignoring this melodrama, their focus on Lazlo Vakraine as he made his way out of the ring and started up the aisle for the locker room, a bounce to his step, adoring the adulation of the happy fans. As he passed the row where Crandall and Paula was sitting, he glanced in their direction and Blackjack saw a gleam in the man's black eyes, a gleam of sadistic satisfaction. Then he was gone. Crandall shivered suddenly then turned back to Paula, who was smiling smugly.

"I know," he said, running fingers through his thick, unruly red hair. "You told me so."

Then he looked back up to the ring in time to see the doctor get to his feet and yell to the referee, "Get an ambulance here! NOW!"

☠ ☠ ☠

In a small, two-bedroom apartment in the seedier part of Cape Noire, a dead man sits in the dark contemplating his past. Alone, upright in an old cushioned strait back chair, he faces the room's only window and stares out at the city. Diffused light from the several streetlamps below illuminate his awful, ravaged features which none have seen without losing their sanity.

He is Brother Bones, the Undead Avenger and the small bed against the wall behind him has never been used. Dead men don't sleep; nor do they dream. As yet, in his mind that continues to function, mental pictures parade through his thoughts constantly. They are the images of all the people he has slain while walking the earth as the mob killer, Thomas 'Tommy' Bonello. He sees them vividly, his memories burn with each moment of terror and horror he instilled in them just as his guns ended their lives. No living man could sustain such a haunting, but Bones is no longer alive. He is trapped in a place between life and death, captured in this ethereal state by the spirits of fate to do their bidding.

For in the end, Tommy Bonello's wanton existence led him to the edge of the eternal abyss and there, looking down into the endless stygian blackness, his conscience was awakened and everything changed. He sought both redemption and penance, but they were cruelly denied him when his twin brother and former partner in the murder trade, Jack Bonello, refused to allow that salvation.

Jack found Tommy living in a coastal monastery and was so outraged, he had his men massacre everyone residing there. Then their bodies were piled into the main building and it was set on fire. Thus ended the hard life of Tommy Bonello. Jack felt absolutely no remorse at all.

Weeks later, while he and two of his men were torturing a young freckled-faced casino employee named Blackjack Bobby Crandall, on orders from their boss, they were set upon by a ghostly wraith. After eliminating the two gunsels, the invisible spirit fell upon Jack and revealed itself as the soul of his murdered brother, Tommy. And then it took its revenge by invading Jack's body and claiming it. The process ended Jack's existence and the body's life force.

Yet, somehow it continued to move and function. Thus did Tommy Bonello come to the grim reality of his new existence. Trapped in his brother's dead body, he had been sent back to the land of the living as agent of retribution to all those who would prey on the innocent. He had been anointed by the karmic forces of the cosmos to be their sword of vengeance.

After releasing the frightened Blackjack Crandall, the undead being demanded his allegiance as the price for his rescue. Having no other option, the young man gave it grudgingly. Later, he was directed to drive the walking zombie killer to the ruins of the old monastery where the bizarre being found a bone white ceramic mask in the ruins. It was sculpted in the shape of a skull. He carefully placed it over his now decaying gray face and from the eye holes peered the black orbs of a dead man.

The birth of Brother Bones was complete.

In the succeeding months, the horrifying figure, draped in a black cloak and slouch hat of the same midnight hue, became the scourge of the underworld. Gang bosses and two-bit killers all became his targets and once on their trail, they were doomed men because Brother Bones was relentless; his blazing silver plated .45 automatic cutting a swathe through the criminal populace of Cape Noire until even the mention of his name caused hardened men to tremble and look over their shoulders into the shadows of the night.

When not hunting the streets on his cursed crusade, Bones sits like a statue at the window of his tiny sanctum, unseeing eyes gazing on the lights of city.

To his left is a bureau and mirror, both layered with dust. On it is a candle stick set in a brass holder and beside it the eerie, ivory ceramic mask.

A tiny gust of air moves the blackened wick and it suddenly ignites, its flame casting dancing shadows over the walls and ceilings. Brother Bones turns, sees the flame and rises. He approaches the tall, thin candle, his watery eyes reflecting its shimmering light and he waits for his summoning.

Slowly, coalescing vaguely in the rising curls of smoke, the face of a young woman begins to shape. The face of a teenage prostitute; the last victim of Tommy Bonello's career. Since his transformation as the Undead Avenger, she has appeared from the void as his spirit guide, manifesting herself only when some horrendous, unorthodox crime has been committed and requires his brand of lethal justice.

Her voice, still sweet and vibrant, addresses him coolly. "An ancient beast has come to Cape Noire."

"What is it and where will I find it?"

"Listen to Blackjack's tale. He will point you to this ageless abomination that feeds on others."

"Stop speaking in circles. Tell me what it is I must find and destroy."

The image began to fade away as she breathed, "Vampire," and the light was snuffed out.

It was shortly after two a.m. when Bobby Crandall walked up the steps to his second floor apartment. There was a lopsided smile on his freckled face as he thought of the sight of Paula Wozcheski naked under the sheets as he'd exited her bedroom. He could still smell the lingering scent of her perfume on his hands and face. Their lovemaking had been exciting and all-consuming, creating a memory he would cherish for a long, long time.

His fingers fumbled his keys into the front door slot as tried to open it quietly. Although he wondered why he even bothered, as his oh-so-weird roommate never slept; or so he claimed. Not that Crandall ever had the nerve to go into that room where the dead man stayed.

Switching on the lights over the tiny kitchenette, he was startled to see Brother Bones sitting at the small square table in full regalia; dirty black overcoat, no doubt concealing his twin under-arm holsters for his twin .45s, his ratty wide brim hat and the unchanging, pure white skull mask.

"Sheesh," he blurted out, "give a guy some warning, will yah?"

"Where have you been?" was all Bones had to offer.

"What's it to you?" Crandall snapped, dropping his keys on the table. "Can't I have a private life while being your stooge and chauffeur?"

The lifeless black eyes bore into him, then the macabre being shook his head slowly. "I don't care about your romantic dalliances. Where were you this evening?"

"At McCoy stadium for the fights, with Paula. Why?"

"Tell me what happened there. Anything out of the ordinary."

Crandall leaned back against the sink and tugged at his chin thoughtfully. "You know, there was a something weird about that last fight; the main event."

THE IMAGE BEGAN TO FADE AWAY AS SHE BREATHED, "VAMPIRE."

"How so?"

"Well this odd-looking guy from overseas, tall and sickly looking, got in the ring with a giant black boxer named Anderson.

"By all odds, Anderson should have mopped up the floor with him. But somehow the other guy, his name was Vakraine, won and tore up Anderson so bad, they had to take him to the hospital. He was still out cold when they carried him out on a stretcher."

"I don't understand. What was so different about it? One guy beats up another. Happens all the time in a fight."

"Not like this, Bones. Look, I don't know if I can explain clearly and maybe it's just my imagination, but…"

"But what?"

"It looked like the stronger this Vakraine got, the weaker Anderson became…like he was sucking up his strength. I told you it was weird. Hell, maybe its my imagination going into overdrive, considering all the things I've seen lately."

Brother Bones nodded. "Where did they take him?"

"St. Mary's hospital, I'd guess. It would be the closest one to the stadium."

The chair was pushed back as the Undead Avenger stood. "Take me there."

"Now?"

The black eyes were unwavering pits of unfathomable horror. "My spirit guide appeared to me, Bobby Crandall, and said a great evil had come to Cape Noire this night."

"Oh, her again, huh?"

"She also said you would lead me to it."

☠ ☠ ☠

Doctor Emil Rayburn took off his horned-rim glasses with his left hand and pinched the bridge of his nose with his right. It was late and he was tired, the harsh glare of the emergency room lights beating down on him were causing a small headache.

He was standing in the central corridor between the main lobby and the triage room where he and the hospital staff had fought futilely to save Jake Anderson. Thinking back on it, he still wasn't sure what had transpired. Somehow, the man's body functions had all systematically shut down; as if someone has shut off a switch going from life to death.

His colleague, Dr. John Wilson, on duty that evening, had been directing the routine procedures but nothing he and his nurses did had any effect. Within twenty minutes of being wheeled into St. Mary's Hospital, the prize-fighter was pronounced dead; cause of death severe trauma to his nervous system most likely sustained during the fight.

Which was pure bullcrap, Doc Rayburn realized. Fancy words to cover up the fact that neither he nor Wilson had any real clue why the healthy black man had died. Rayburn had been a ring-side pysician for six years and in that time had dealt with all manner of injuries men inflicted on each other while in ring. He had thought he'd seen it all, until this unexplainable fatality.

He had also done his duty in supporting Doctor Wilson when the man had to go out to the waiting room where Anderson's wife and parents had assembled shortly after he was brought to the hospital. The look of pain and suffering on their weary faces was something he would never forget; the young Mrs. Anderson falling to her knees, tears streaming down her face. It had taken the two of them almost an hour to deal with them as officially and compassionately as was humanly possible.

After being allowed to view the body, Wilson had ushered the family to the front door, explaining that the body would be moved to their morgue until plans could be made with a local mortuary to pick it up the next morning. Once done, he and his crew headed for the second floor cafeteria to grab some coffee and sandwiches. Rayburn had declined the invitation to join them, seeing the lateness of the hour and begged off.

Now, alone in the corridor, all he wanted to do was retrieve his medical kit and go home. He remembered setting it aside in the triage room when the ambulance drivers had wheeled in their gurney on which the comatose Anderson was strapped. He walked back to that closed door and pushed it open.

The last person to leave the room, after the family had said their goodbyes, had turned off the lights, so he now reached out to switch them back on rather then go stumbling around in the dark. A guttural noise from the operating table caught him by surprise.

There, under the glaring florescent light, was easily the strangest sight Emil Rayburn had ever seen. A man, dressed in dark clothing, was crouched over Jake Anderson's body. The white sheet that had covered the corpse had been pulled back and the fellow on the body was leaning down over the face, his big hands holding open the dead man's mouth with his own leaning close to those cold lips.

"What the hell is this?" Rayburn blurted, surprised and scared at the same time. "Get off that body!"

The cruel-looking man, sat up and wiped his own mouth with the back of his hand, a sneer across his face. "Gladly. This one is empty now and I still hunger."

Doctor Rayburn took a step back feeling for the door, just then the stranger leaped off the corpse in his direction. Without another look back, the middle-aged healer ripped the door open and flung himself out of the room. He could hear the man laughing behind him and realized he was in real danger. Whoever that lunatic was, he meant to do him serious harm, of that he had no doubt. Head twisting, he knew going towards the lobby was too far a run, whereas spinning to the left, he sighted the exit door to the back parking lot only twenty yards away.

As he ran for it, Rayburn heard shuffling feet behind him and knew the crazy man was right behind him. His fear-riddled mind was praying to the Almighty, as his chest heaved and his feet kept racing forward.

Then he was at the exit pushing the steel bar to throw it open. Cool night air filled his lungs as he gulped moving over the cement platform and down the three steps to the tarred lot.

Everything was happening so fast. He heard the door behind being struck hard, he saw the area ahead was nearly deserted of automobiles or anyone who could possibly help him and he kept running. In the distance he thought he heard an approaching car but he couldn't see it.

Suddenly there was a hideous, shrill cry and a heavy weight fell on his back driving him to the unyielding ground. His palms were ripped, as were his knees, through his corduroy trousers as he feebly tried to break his fall. Then he was flat on his stomach, knees pushing down on his back, while a pair of hands groped for his head and began to pull it back.

"Foolish man, there is no escape for cattle when our kind hunts," the harsh voice spoke into his left ear. Rayburn could smell a fetid stench and desperately tried to rise, but the weight was too heavy and the hands on his head began to increase their pressure.

There were two loud explosions and Rayburn's attacker was flung across the ground like a torn rag doll.

The doctor turned his eyes and beheld as yet another out-of-this-world picture. A roadster stood parked in the middle of the empty parking area, its engine idling. Standing in front of the open passenger side door was Brother Bones, clad in his dark clothing, his gloved hands wrapped around his twin .45 automatics, tiny wisps of smoke curling from their barrels. His masked visage gruesome to behold under the brim of his hat.

"Get the machete," Bones ordered Bobby Crandall, seated behind the steering wheel.

Believing he was living some twisted nightmare, Rayburn started to get off the ground, his palms smarting as the grit dug into the soft flesh. Feeling a bit dizzy, he stood as the Undead Avenger approached him.

"Are you alright?"

"I think so. You're that…ah…vigilante they write about in the papers; Brother Bones."

"We haven't much time. What happened here? Who is that man?"

"I don't know," Rayburn replied still dazed. "He was in the operating table, sitting on Mr. Anderson's body as if he wanted to…kiss it. God, I sound crazy."

"These are crazy times," rasped Bones as he moved towards the still moving body of the man he had shot.

The fellow on the ground had rolled over onto his side and was attempting to sit up despite the two holes in his chest. He saw Brother Bones and spit at him. "I will rip your heart out and eat it!" he threatened, spittle moistening his lips.

"You're too late," Bones said standing over him. "I know what you are."

"Then you know we are immortal."

"Wrong."

Brother Bones lowered the guns in his hands and fired four more round, the last into the man's head tearing off half his scalp. The booming blasts echoed through open space.

"Geezus!" Blackjack gasped as he came up to Bones, a heavy, sharp machete in his hands.

Bones ignored his comment, holstered his weapons, took hold of the machete and then knelt down beside his victim and hacked off his head. Rising, he handed Crandall the bloody blade and started for the now shocked Doctor Rayburn.

"We have to go," he explained. Rayburn couldn't take his eyes off the mangled head in Bones'hand. "You must come with us."

"What? Huh! Why?"

Brother Bones twisted his head towards the headless body behind them. "You don't want to be here when the police arrive."

"But…"

"I don't have time for this, doctor."

Crandall had tossed the machete into the car's trunk and was back behind the wheel looking out at Bones and the traumatized Rayburn.

In the distance there arose the faint sound of sirens.

"Doctor?" Bones raised the timber of his voice and the man blinked. He looked at the snow white mask, the bottomless black eyes behind it and shivered. What choice did he really have?

"Very well," he mumbled.

Brother Bones took hold of his arm and ushered him to the front passenger side. Once Rayburn was seated, he slammed the door shut and hurriedly climbed into the back seat.

He dropped the wet severed head onto the floorboard and ordered Blackjack Bobby Crandall to step on it.

The speedy automobile drove through the nearly deserted streets of Cape Noire passing an occasional business truck such as those delivering the morning editions of the Tribune. In a few hours twilight would creep over the city and a new day would dawn.

But for the riders in this vehicle, the last vestiges of the old day were still being played out.

"So who are you?" Rayburn finally asked the freckle-faced man behind the wheel.

"He's not important," Brother Bones spoke, leaning forward from the back seat, a firm hand on the doctor's shoulder. "I need you to tell me everything you witnessed at the hospital, Doctor…"

"Emil Rayburn. That's my name."

"Please, Doctor Rayburn. I need to know exactly what it is that happened there."

"Very well. It all began when Anderson collapsed in the ring at the stadium…"

And so the weary physician related his tale. The first half was his version of what Crandall had already reported to Bones. It was the moments he had experienced in the hospital that had the Undead Avenger's rapt attention.

"He seemed to have his mouth over Anderson's," Rayburn said, the image coming back to him vividly.

"He was sucking the rest of him dry," Brother Bones explained.

"Dry? I don't understand. What exactly does that mean?"

"It means the man who defeated Anderson did so by draining his life essences. This Lazlo Vakraine is a vampire."

"A vampire!" Rayburn turned his head to Bones. "That is preposterous. There are no such things."

"And aren't they supposed to bite people on the neck and suck their blood?" Blackjack interrupted. "You know, like Bela Lugosi in the movies."

"If we're to believe myths and legends," Brother Bones continued. "But what if, throughout the centuries this monster has survived, he continued to evolve. Enough so that he no longer has to savage his victims, but can actually drain their life force by coming into close physical proximity to them."

"You mean, like in a fight," Rayburn offered, having a hard time believing he was even participating in such a conversation.

"Hey, wait a second!" Blackjack exclaimed. "That's it. That's where I saw that guy before."

"What guy?" Bones asked.

"The one who jumped the doc, here. Mister Head you got back there."

"You've seen him before, Crandall?"

"Yes. At the fights. He was one of Vakraine's ring crew!"

☻ ☻ ☻

They drove Doctor Rayburn to his home and then Brother Bones directed Bobby Crandall to take them to the nearest docks along the port city's wharves. Pink and orange rays were coloring the heavens by the time they arrived. A few longshoremen could be seen in the distance reporting for work.

Bones climbed out of the back seat with the severed head in his hands, stepped to the end of the wooden dock and dropped it into the ocean. There was a sizzling sound as the purifying properties of the salt ate at the tainted object and dissolved it like a fast-acting acid.

Back in the front passenger seat, Brother Bones gave Crandall new directives as they drove away.

"Take us home, wash and get some sleep. You are going to need it."

"I don't like the sound of that. What have you got planned."

"Not a plan as such, but simply preparations' that need doing before we confront Vakraine."

"Such as?"

"I will leave a list on the table. When you awaken, read it and obtain the items I'll have listed there."

"Such as?"

"The obvious, of course. Holy water and wooden stakes."

"Oh."

"Among other things."

☻ ☻ ☻

For a Thursday night, the Gray Owl Casino was jumping. The popular gambling house/night club was packed with people all shoving each other from one gaming table to another. In the lounge room, located at the back of the club, soft jazz music was being played by an all black band and was all but drowned out by the chatter of the enthusiastic chance takers.

The table with the most activity was that of Blackjack Bobby Crandall, the freckle-faced redhead with the affable personality. Folks just naturally gravitated to the smiling card dealer and he always did his best to make them feel welcome regardless of their luck or lack-of on any particular evening. His game, like his name, was blackjack.

For his part, Crandall relished the loud ebb and flow of crowd mixed with new and old familiar faces alike. After the events of the previous night, he considered his job the one sane haven left to him.

It had been a long day for the young man. After catching six hours of sleep, he'd grabbed a burger at a local diner before running the errands Brother Bones demanded. On his return to his apartment, he'd picked up the afternoon edition of the Cape Noir Tribune and scanned it for any stories relating to their nocturnal activities. The news of Big Bear Anderson's death was top—heading on the sports page, attributing cause of death to a heart attack. Whereas the police blotter on page two had a single column devoted to the headless remains of an unidentified male found behind St.Mary's Hospital. Crandall had circled both stories with a pencil and left the paper on the kitchen table along with the items he'd purchased for Brother Bones.

Now, after two hours of non-stop dealing, he was about to call the Pit Boss, Greg Landers, and request a fifteen minute break when he saw Paula Wozcheski pushing through the crowd in her sexy cigarette-girl's outfit of high heels, fishnet stockings and a lacy black bustier that did wonders to her long legged, statuesque figure. Her shiny black tresses were piled up in a bun atop her head and she looked incredibly beautiful.

Even with her box-tray of cigarettes and cigars draped around her neck, she was managing to hold onto a big ceramic mug filled with steaming black coffee. Moving around the corner of his table, she sidled up beside him and carefully handed him the cup.

"Here, I thought you could use this along about now," she explained, a sparkle in her eyes.

"Thanks," Crandall returned, holding his deck in his right hand and grabbing the mug with his left. He took a slow, generous swallow. It was strong just the way he liked it. The rich caffeine instantly flooding through his body was just the jolt he needed.

Standing so close to Paula, he could smell her rose scented perfume and he was reminded of their fiery intimacy the previous evening, before everything else had gone wacko. They had only managed to say a few words to each other upon arriving at the casino shortly before the place opened and now both seemed to be sharing the same pleasing memory.

"Hey, kid, how about a card?" a beefy man with a bulbous nose grumbled across the velvet topped table. Before him were two cards face up, a ten and a five; fifteen points. To win he needed a six or less.

"Hold your horses," Crandall smiled and put down his mug. He pinched the next card off the top of the deck and flipped it down on the other three. It was a seven. "Busted, my friend," he stated the obvious.

"Damn it," the man cursed. His stack of plastic chips was quickly dwindling.

"You should have been a bit more patient," Crandall suggested. "Lady Luck doesn't like to be hurried."

"Hardy, har, har," the patron groused, counting off another fifty dollars worth of chips and setting them in the middle of the table. "Come on, let's do it again."

Crandall leaned towards Paula's ear and whispered, "Some people never learn."

She laughed, turned her head and gave him a little kiss on the cheek. "I'd better get back to work too. See you later."

The lovely brunette had just disappeared into the crowd when Blackjack heard a boisterous commotion coming from the main lobby. Over the heads of those around him, he could see the noise was centered on a group of new arrivals that had clearly excited the throng in the hall. He assumed some big shot politician or celebrity had just made an appearance as was commonplace. This was, after all, the swankest joint in town.

Then he heard someone call, "Hey, it's that boxer from Bavaria!" Bobby Crandall was caught off guard. This was the last place he would have expected to see the man Brother Bones labeled a vampire. And sure enough, there he was, Lazlo Vakraine, moving through a group of admirers looking as if he were some distinguished foreign prince. Attired in a black tuxedo, with a white carnation in his lapel, his dark hair slicked back, the famous fighter was clearly enjoying the attention he was receiving. Of course he was also not alone, three of his comrades were following behind him and even though dressed in respectable, fancy suits, they still looked liked hired thugs.

Blackjack Crandall was momentarily confused as to what he should do. After all, the guy was a monster; but he was the only one who knew that. Were he to make any kind of accusation, here of all places, he'd not only be laughed at as a nut but most likely be fired. No, logic dictated he do nothing to let Vakraine know he was on to him. He mentally counted to ten, took another drink of coffee and let his nerves calm down.

Of course it was his table that the "Bruiser From Bavaria" chose to visit.

As several of his regulars moved apart to make room for the gaunt, charismatic foreigner, Crandall stopped dealing and looked directly into the man's eyes. There was a brief glimmer of recognition.

"I know you," Lazlo Vakraine said in a thick accented voice.

"I was at the fight," Crandall acknowledged, trying to sound normal and friendly. "I saw you beat Anderson."

"Ah, yes," Vakraine gestured, placing his right hand over his heart. "Such an awful tragedy. I was crushed upon hearing the news. It is one of the risks for our…ah…sport."

For a moment no one said a word, the men and women around them obviously uncomfortable with the awkward topic of death interrupting their fun. Still, Crandall could see there was something about Vakraine that held them all enthralled and he truly believed he was an unholy being that posed a threat to everyone present. Despite his many adventures with the Undead Avenger, Crandall never once sensed anything but a true force for justice in the skull-masked zombie.

Not so in the presence of Lazlo Vakraine. All that eminated from the man was a feeling of pure evil.

"What is this game you play?" Vakraine asked, a cold smile on his eagle-like features.

"It's called twenty-one or Blackjack. The object is to…"

"I know it," Vakraine nodded. "I was taught while in Monte Carlo. Is there room for me?"

Crandall was going to reply no when the fat man piped up. "Hey, you can have my spot, buddy. Time for me to quit anyway."

"Thank you." Vakraine turned to one of his men, a bald-headed, stocky fellow with an ugly red scar crossing his right cheek. "Chips, Otto." The fellow dug into his jacket pocket and handed him five hundred dollars worth of tokens.

Vakraine put down a fifty dollar red chip, looked at Crandall and said, "A card, please."

☠ ☠ ☠

The next thirty minutes were the most aggravating and nervous minutes Bobby Crandall ever had to endure. The European boxer was lucky and though he lost a few deals, for the most part he easily doubled his money effortlessly.

At the same time his flamboyant, egregious personality continued to attract more and more people to the table until there were at least one hundred revelers watching him play. Crandall was starting to feel claustrophobic with all those bodies pressing in around them, their phony, greedy smiles trying to absorb some of the Bavarian's charm and luck. God, mused Blackjack, if they only knew his true face.

Then, just when he thought he couldn't go on another minute, Vakraine tossed him a fifty dollar chip, gathered up his winnings and handed them to his aid, Otto. "This has been most enjoyable, young man. My thanks."

"You're a lucky man," Crandall admitted, keeping his voice neutral as he pocketed the chip.

"I am indeed," Vakraine chuckled. He turned and raised his arms outward, facing his fans. "And I wish to share my good fortune with any of you willing to join me at my suite at the Chandler Arms hotel for a party. There will be much champagne and caviar. Yes?"

At least half a dozen women squealed in delight as they nudged their husbands or boyfriends to accept Vakraine's unexpected invitation. Without a backward look at Crandall, the self-assured Bavarian walked off, now trailed by a bunch of happy citizens who all thought they'd just hit the jackpot.

Bobby Crandall watched them walk out of the main room towards the front lobby and shook his head. They were like sheep walking numbly off to the slaughter house. But even if he tried to warn them, he doubted any of them would listen. His only course of action was to finish his shift, then hurry home and report to Brother Bones. Now that he knew where Vakraine was staying, the Undead Avenger would take care of the rest. He only hoped they would be in time.

☠ ☠ ☠

The remainder of the evening was a torturous, routine affair for Bobby Crandall. He kept glancing at his wristwatch, silently begging for time to speed up. After midnight, the regular patrons had cleared out and only a few of the diehard gambling addicts remained, wandering from table to table in search of that winners' euphoria they could never hold on to.

By the time Greg Landers began making the table circuits telling everyone to count-up and turn in their chips, Crandall was ready to bolt. He did a quick tally of his remaining chips, jotted it down on a slip of yellow paper and threw it into a green money bag along with the tokens. He delivered the bag to the bank window, signed a receipt log with the amount total and then he was finished.

His plan was to pick up Paula at the hat-check counter next to the front entrance, take her home and then join up with Brother Bones as planned. Unfortunately, amidst the group of employees moving swiftly through the vestibule, he didn't spot his girlfriend among them. Confused, he moved to the front counter where Nancy Glass, a pretty blond, was locking up the now empty closet room.

"Hey, Nancy," he said coming up behind her. "Where's Paula? Is she in the lady's room?"

"Oh, no," the blue eyed girl answered. "She took off early with that crowd going to that boxer's party."

"What? You mean that foreigner, Vakraine?"

"Right. He spotted her on his way out and stopped to flirt with her."

"What?"

"Geez, Blackjack, what's your problem? You really that jealous?"

Crandall lowered his voice. "Alright, sorry. So what happened... exactly?"

"Well, this guy suggested Paula get off work and come to his big shindig at the Chandler. After he'd left, she went to see the boss and he told her she could clock out early. And that's what she did."

Crandall was stunned. Paula was with that monster! All the while he'd been dealing cards as if nothing were wrong.

"She did ask me to tell you," the blonde added. "She said to tell you that you should meet her there when you got off."

"Right." Suddenly he was sick to his stomach.

"See, you ain't got nothing to worry about. She's only got eyes for you, Blackjack."

Crandall didn't hear the end of the girl's reassurance; he was already running for the front door. The thoughts racing through his mind were frightening.

☠ ☠ ☠

"Slow down, Crandall!" Brother Bones commanded as the roadster took the street corner at a breakneck speed, shoving him against the front passenger door hard. The roadster's chassis leaned precariously to the right threatening to pull the left side rubber off the road. "Crashing us will not help your girlfriend!"

Bobby Crandall, clutching the steering wheel like a life preserver in a sea storm, glared back Bones. "No! She's in that monster's hands and it's all my fault."

"It will also be your fault when you drive us into the gutter and end this mad chase, and your life. Then how well do you think the girl will fare?"

Frustrated in having no answer to his master's logic, Crandall began to ease off the gas pedal and the car straightened out as it continued racing towards the heart of the downtown district. The Chandler Arms was the poshest hotel in Cape Noire and was located in the center of the sprawling port metropolis.

"Do you really think these religious trinkets will work?" Crandall changed topics, clutching the silver crucifix Bones had handed him minutes earlier as they left his apartment. The Undead Avenger, as was most often the case these days, had been sitting at the kitchen table when he rushed home. On the table before him was a bag with several medals on chains and a dark-colored bottle filled with Holy Water from St. Michael's Catholic church and a several boxes of shotgun shells and bullets. Bones had spent most of the early evening painting the ammunition with the blessed water.

"We are battling soulless creatures who don't know the meaning of hope and faith. That is their weakness; their one vulnerability. Any belief system is stronger than their lack of such."

"So you're telling me a Star of David would be just as effective?"

"Yes. The type of faith is immaterial. Simply having faith is what will save you."

"What about you?"

Brother Bones chuckled. It sounded like sandpaper brushing against a post. "I'm dead, Crandall. No one can save me now."

☠ ☠ ☠

The majestic, fifteen story Chandler Arms appeared before them like a man-made mountain, towering above all the other buildings on the block. At Bones' orders, Crandall drove them past the ornate façade, the front awning entrance and around to the back of the edifice where a darkened alley provided access to delivery trucks needing to service and supply the grand hotel. He pulled up alongside a steel dumpster and shut off the engine.

Once out of the car, they went to the trunk and from it procured Brother Bones' machete, which he tied with a cord under his left arm, leaving his hands free to wield his big .45 automatic. Then he stuffed extra gun clips into his overcoat pockets at the same time Bobby Crandall was pulling a twelve-gauge shotgun from the trunk. Taking the brown bag from Bones, he filled his own jacket pockets with two dozen jacketed shotgun rounds.

Together, side by side, they marched to the hotel's back door service entrance. A small light bulb hanging over the door lit the cement ramp and stoop.

Crandall cast his eyes upwards. "How are we going to find which room they're in?"

"Leave that to me," Brother Bones replied as they started up the steps. "Once I've encountered a threat, I can sense it anywhere. The thing at the hospital had a particular essence which I'll recognize as we approach it."

"If you say so."

The door was unlocked and once opened, they entered a brightly-lit corridor. They could hear noises coming from various rooms down the hall where the skeletal night staff was moving around. To their immediate left was a door marked STAIRS. Brother Bones nodded and Crandall shoved it open. Without hesitation, the Undead Avenger started upwards, the redhead coming up behind him, his weapon held at ready against his chest.

Ten minutes later they were rounding the door to the tenth floor and Brother Bones stopped. He stood statue like for a few seconds, then grabbed the doorknob. "They are on this floor."

Crandall's throat was dry as he moved hurriedly behind Bones, who was quickly going down the empty corridor looking intently from door-to-door. At the third door, he came to a halt and whipped out his automatics. He turned to look at his protégé, his dull black eyes conveying their obvious warning. Blackjack merely nodded once and jerked a round into the firing chamber of his shotgun. He was as ready as he would ever be.

Brother Bones banged on the door with the butt of the .45 in his right hand and then waited.

Eerily there was no noise coming from behind the door. Crandall nervously realized how wrong that was. A party with over a dozen rowdy men and women and not a single peep.

There was a shuffling noise suddenly and Bones took a step back and put the tip of his pistol against the eye-hole in the door. There was a muffled query from inside and he squeezed the trigger. The bullet tore a fist size gap in the wooden portal with a loud boom followed by an agonizing scream.

Brother Bones slammed his right shoulder into the door, breaking it open and there stood one of Vakraine's flunkies, holding a bloody hand over the ruined left side of his face. Seeing Bones, he snarled, "Bastard!" His mouth revealed blood stained fangs as he mindlessly attacked.

Brother Bones put two more shots into the wounded man's chest propelling his body backwards into the lower level main room. At the same time, Bobby Crandall had edged his way around the Undead Avenger and charged forward to see the flying man come crashing down on the back of a long couch. Ready for anything, the card dealer was unprepared for the surreal scene stretched out before him.

Over a dozen men and women, some whom he recognized from the club, were scattered all over the room, most of them naked and unmoving, their bodies blood-smeared, their faces frozen in twisted, grotesque grimaces. Moving among them were Lazlo Vakraine's three remaining stooges, not counting the unlucky fellow who had encountered the Undead Avenger at the front door.

Two were stretched out beside the bodies of young women, licking the blood red splatters over their breasts, while the third sat on a padded chair, a half-dressed woman on his lap sucking on her neck. Her half-closed eyes looked at Crandall standing there and she softly pleaded, "Help me."

Her attacker looked up, his lips smeared rouge and his eyes, also the same hue, widened at the sight of the armed intruder. With a sneer, he pushed the half-dead woman onto the carpeted floor and sprang to his feet. In the blink of an eye, he launched himself across the room, arms out. Blackjack's mind registered the fiend's hands reaching for him, the nails suddenly growing into pointed claws.

He turned the shotgun around and fired. The blast hit the vampire directly, tearing off half his face before spinning him around in midair and dropping him into a coffee table covered with empty beer bottles, glasses and ashtrays. It broke into thousands of pieces under the thing's weight.

Unprepared for the suddenness of the assaults, Crandall hadn't been ready and the recoil of the weapon's wooden stock slammed into his chest knocking the wind out of his lungs.

The other two undead Bavarians were quickly rising to their feet, their bodies beginning to morph into the same animal features of the man he'd shot. The same man who was now moving amongst the debris of the smashed table, shards of glass stuck in his arms and torso. He turned his half mangled face towards Crandall and cried out in primal rage.

Suddenly curls of smoke erupted over his damaged features which soon became snapping flames eating away the demolished skin.

The monster screamed in agony and began beating his head with his hands.

"It's the Holy Water on the pellets," Brother Bones informed, coming up beside Crandall with something in his hands. Crandall glanced down and saw the head of the man who had come to the door.

"Here, catch!" Bones blurted, tossing the gruesome object across the room to the nearest vampire who instinctively caught it before being aware of what it was.

At the same time, the Undead Avenger whipped up his right arm and shot the startled vampire three times in the chest.

"Keep shooting, Crandall. We're not out of the woods yet."

Bobby Crandall watched his macabre master move after the remaining blood-sucker still on his feet and turned his own attention back to the gyrating fiend before him. The fire on the monster's face was still consuming him. Crandall close the gap between them, pointed the shotgun at the burning head and blew it away. Plumes of smoke curled up from the neck aperture, as did fountains of crimson gore and blood.

Meanwhile, Bones had taken out the third and final killer and, unfastening his machete, started in with his decapitations again.

In a daze, smelling pungent cordite gunsmoke, Crandall watched his headless foe topple over and he took a moment to catch his breath. Slowly he surveyed both the horror scenario they had invaded and the carnage he and Brother Bones had added to it. He moved among some of the naked victims and was shocked to discover all were not dead.

"Bones, some of these people are still alive!"

"Yes, I know. I'm sure by now someone has notified the front desk about the gunfire."

Crandall ran a shaky hand through his hair. "I thought they only sucked out life energy like that creep at the hospital. What the hell is going on here?"

"Merely a time-honored, ancient ritual," another voice entered the conversation. It was Lazlo Vakraine, standing bare-chested in the doorway behind Bones, a dangerous smile on his face. "My followers were not as evolved and could only sustain themselves via their animal lust."

Brother Bones stood erect, a .45 in one hand and his blood coated machete in the other. Red drops sprinkled his bone-white mask. He and Lazlo Vakraine took the measure of each other.

"You must be the one they call Brother Bones," the Bavarian acknowledged. "I confess, I thought you were just another American boogie man fairy tale. I am impressed."

"And soon you will be dead," Bones started towards the regal vampire, only to have him disappear into the dark bedroom behind him.

Bobby Crandall rushed after Bones and both of them entered the adjacent room together. The only light came from an open window along the back wall. Feeling Crandall come up behind him, Bones put up his hand to hold him back. They could be walking into a clever trap.

"Show yourself, Vakraine."

"Gladly, my friend." Suddenly the tall, lithe Vakraine appeared in front of the open window dragging someone before him. In the feeble light cast from the living room, it was clearly a struggling female.

As Lazlo Vakraine pulled her up before him like a shield, Bobby Crandall gasped. "Paula!"

"Ah, yes, the young card dealer," recognition in his voice. "It would seem you have a vested interest in this amusing little affair." He was holding Paula around the waist with his left arm, her mouth was gagged with a piece of cloth and her hands were apparently tied behind her back. Her eyes were terror-filled as the vampire lord touched her cheek caressingly with his long fingers. "She is a very beautiful woman, is she not?"

"Let her go!" Crandall demanded.

"Oh, and why should I do that?" Vakraine retorted. "After all, she is my, how do you Americans say it…ah, yes: My ace in the hole."

"Would you fight for her?" Brother Bones inquired. "Or are you a coward behind your cultured ego?"

"You would challenge me to a boxing contest?"

"Yes. Me and you, alone in the ring, without any weapons. Just our fists to settle this thing."

Lazlo Vakraine laughed, relishing the idea. "Very well, Brother Bones. We will meet in the ring at the stadium in one hour. Yes?"

"I'll be there."

Vakraine looked back over his shoulder, then climbed out the window

LAZLO VAKRAINE PULLED HER UP BEFORE HIM LIKE A SHIELD.

onto the wrought iron balcony, dragging the squirming woman with him. "Do not disappoint me or the girl will suffer."

Then he leapt over the railing with his prisoner.

"NO!" cried Bobby Crandall, pushing past Bones to get to the window. Climbing out onto the balcony, he was in time to see the vampire in human guise hurtle over through space to land on the roof of the next building, which was a few stories shorter. He did so effortlessly, the woman now slung over his shoulder. Then Vakraine looked back at Crandall and Bones, gave them a jaunty salute and ran off into the darkness.

💀 💀 💀

Brother Bones walked down the center aisle of McCoy Stadium, his footsteps echoing through the spacious, nearly deserted venue. The only lights on were those above the ring where Lazlo Vakraine awaited him. The vampire boxer was still shirtless, dressed only in black slacks, socks and shoes.

Upon seeing Bones, the dark-haired Bavarian clapped gently. "Excellent," he called out so Bones could hear. "I was beginning to think you would not come."

Offering no response, the Undead Avenger of Cape Noire continued down the path amidst the thousands of empty seats. There was a prevalent, cemetery-like atmosphere without the people who normally filled those chairs.

Reaching the bottom, Brother Bones saw one chair at the center of the front row was occupied. There, lying still, gag still in place, stretched Paula Wozcheski. Bones went to inspect her condition and, standing over her, could see her chest rising and falling. She was only asleep. Then he saw the twin, blood caked holes on the side of he neck.

"I only took a small taste," Lazlo Vakraine explained, having moved to the ropes behind Bones and now looking down over his shoulder. "I'm sure you can understand."

"Will she live?" Bones turned to look at him.

"That is for you to decide, is it not?"

Black, dead eyes look into pools equally stygian, only vibrant with a fiery, endless hunger.

Brother Bones removed his slouch hat and overcoat. He laid them on the seat beside the unconscious girl, then began un-strapping his twin shoulder holsters.

"Where is your young ally?" Vakraine inquired as he began shadow boxing around the ring, in readiness for the coming battle.

"Guarding the front entrance," Bones' raspy voice replied. "I don't want anyone interrupting us 'till this is over."

It was a lie.

"A wise move, my friend."

Bones placed his guns and rig across his clothes, then turned to face the ring once again. "I am not your friend."

Brother Bones took hold of his mask and removed it carefully and set it on the rest of his gear. Then his gloved hands reached up, took hold of the bottom rope and he pulled himself up onto the mat. Pushing down the next middle rope, he slipped under it into the ring proper and stood tall.

Lazlo Vakraine had ceased his shadow boxing and now gazed upon the naked, lifeless face of Brother Bones; a sight that drove normal men crazy.

"My, my, but how ugly you are," he commented. "A true monster, like myself."

Bones remained silent. Such taunts and jeers had no meaning to him. He knew what he was.

Vakraine hustled over to the opposite corner where two pairs of boxing gloves were hanging on the top rope. He pulled a pair free and held them up. "Yes or no?"

"You're kidding, right?"

"Yes, of course," Vakraine agreed, tossing the gloves out of the ring. "After all, this is no game between us."

The Bruiser From Bazaria put up his fists, holding them before his torso and attacked.

Bones turned his body at an angle and blocked the first set of punches. But Vakraine was fast and agile, and he danced away before the grim avenger could retaliate with counter-punches. Brother Bones held his own fists up, body in balanced stance, ready for the next barrage.

It came quickly, Vakraine throwing caution to the wind, pushed himself into Bones and delivered several fast combinations to the dead man's body. Then he slipped a hard left past Bone's arm and hit him square in the head. Bones was thrown back several steps off balance. Not allowing him to fight back, Vakraine pressed his onslaught and two hard blows connected with Bone's head, the last dropping him back against the ropes.

The vampire backed away, a smirk on his face. "Come now, I thought you were going to offer me a true challenge. You move like an old man. Come, fight!"

Brother Bones twisted his misshapen head to crack his neck and raised his fists once more. "You forget, I don't feel pain." He walked back to the center of the ring ready to continue.

Frustrated, Lazlo Vakraine renewed his attack.

At the same time, a hundred and twenty feet above the stadium floor, Blackjack Bobby Crandall moved carefully along the narrow catwalks that had been installed below the massive roof during the stadium's construction. These were used by maintenance crews primarily for two purposes; the first to change the overhead lights when they burned out and the second to open and close the thirty foot long skylight during balmy summer nights.

During their ride over, Brother Bones had detailed all this to his young aid, explaining how in his career as hired killer, he had spent a great deal of time at the arena and had become very well acquainted with its layout, top to bottom. The skylight was a feature rarely used and thus most people were unaware it even existed. Now, if Bones could pull off his part of the plan, it would prove to be Lazlo Vakraine's undoing.

Right, thought Crandall, as he clutched the rope railing and moved along ever so slowly, keeping his eyes front. The glow from the powerful lights suspended ten feet below him afforded him enough illumination to proceed to where Bones had said the control levers were located. At same time they effectively hid him from view. Even the vampire, should he gaze upward, would not be able to penetrate the glare of those harsh lights. Still, Crandall had to assume all of Vakraine's senses were magnified, including that of hearing. Thus he moved along like a church mouse, ever so cautiously, fear his invisible companion.

Without looking down, he could hear Bones and Vakraine punching away at each other and he wondered if his master would be able to keep it up. They still had another hour to go.

In the ring, both supernatural beings continued to pound away at each other relentlessly. The Bavarian vampire's footwork had slowed down considerably, as he came to realize it made no difference against the zombie avenger. Brother Bones, unlike Vakraine's human opponents, was incapable of feeling pain. More importantly, whatever energies fueled his dead body were beyond his abilities to leech.

"You've stayed alive robbing others of theirs," Brother Bones accused as the two men circled each other after another brief but brutal contact, having exchanged several blows. "You cannot take from me what I do not possess."

Lazlo Vakraine's face was cut and bleeding in several places. He sneered and spat on the floor to clear his mouth. It was evident he was tiring. "It matters not; I've existed for over six hundred years and have survived every threat put before me. Even God is afraid of me."

"Ha, ha, ha," Bones laughed coldly. "You are so full of yourself, Vakraine, but the truth is you are a coward."

"And what am I afraid off, you obscene pig?"

"Death. That's why you've run away from it all this time."

And once again both combatants went at each other with a primal fury that had no limits. Blow after blow continued to strike each fighter as time seemed to stand still. For both of them, existence beyond the ring became an illusion and their only imperative reality became defeating the other.

Then the vampire began to change, his features taking on a grimmer appearance, his ears becoming noticeably pointed, his eyes taking on a reddish cast and his incisors began to lengthen into fangs. He was reverting to his true, monstrous form in a purely subconscious attempt to stave off the unstoppable Brother Bones.

"Ah, and now your true, pitiful self comes to the surface as the beast you truly are," Bones taunted.

In response, Vakraine opened his fists to reveal razor sharp claws and began to swipe at the Undead Avenger. His long nails tore Bone's sleeves to shreds as he held up his arms to ward them off, feeling them rip into his cold, lifeless gray flesh.

Suddenly there came a loud mechanical noise from overhead and Brother Bones knew the time to end things had arrived. Considering Vakraine's transformation; not a moment too soon. Now it was critical he keep the fiend occupied a few minutes more.

Bones dropped his guard and moved in, fists hammering at the vampire like the pistons of a locomotive. Punch after punch rocked Vakraine back into a corner exactly where Bones wanted him.

More sounds reached them from the ceiling and through the battering Bones was administering, Lazlo Vakraine finally became aware of it. His head looked up and his eyes doubled in shock.

Filtering through the glare of the powerful overhead lights was a single beam of sunlight.

"No!" he gasped as the narrow band of light began to swell wider and wider as the skylight was cranked open above them. High above, Bobby

Crandall had found the winch and at the agreed upon time began to turn it.

It was six a.m. and sunrise. The ray from outdoors, now sweeping over all of Cape Noire, flooded down into the stadium, spilling into an ever widening pool over the ring.

The vampire went beserk understanding how he had been duped and his complete vulnerability. Frantically, he tried to push off Brother Bones, completely moving beyond any pretense of fighting. His only thought now was escape from that rapidly encroaching light. His claws raked Bones, but the Undead Avenger refused to be moved.

In sheer desperation, Lazlo Vakraine twisted around in an attempt to climb the ropes and get away. Bones immediately reached out and grabbed him around the chest in a tightening hug.

"Let me go!" Wailed Vakraine.

Maintaining his hold, Brother Bones pulled the mad creature out of the corner and dragged him backwards into the middle of the ring where the pillar of light was the brightest.

The second the light touched Vakraine, his skin began to blister. He cried all the louder as more and more of his exposed arms, torso, and head began to sizzle like bacon on a grill. The stench rose off him in curls of yellow smoke and then he was suddenly ablaze. His body burned like a living torch as he continued to contort, every ounce of strength struggling to free himself from the agonizing blaze that consumed him.

For his part, Brother Bones merely stood unmoving, his hold never wavering, though his arms and chest were being singed by the powerful flames and he had to turn his face away to avoid the worst of them.

Within minutes, he felt Vakraine's body collapse in his arms, and a white hot skeleton broke apart in his grasp and crumbed to the mat where it instantly disintegrated into a pile of ashes.

The vampire Lazlo Vakraine was no more.

The battle over, Brother Bones tore off what remained of his white shirt and used the fragments to pat out the flames on his bare arms. He climbed out of the ring where he had left his outer garments and guns only to find that Paula Wozcheski was gone. On the seat where he had observed her sleeping were the gag and ropes that had bound her.

Bones jumped off the mat, went over to where his stuff was and saw that his slouch hat and overcoat were missing. All that remained were his pistols and white skull mask. As he took the skeleton-sculptured disguise and placed it over his face, he surveyed the empty stadium. A quick flutter of movement near the corner of an alcove exit caught his attention and he knew it was the girl. She was hiding from the light.

"Keep the hat and coat," he spoke loudly, while picking up the leather holsters with his pistols. "Try to stay in the shadows until you are home safe."

He waited to see if she would reply. She did not.

"I'm sorry I could not save you, and because of that I will not come after you, Paula Wozcheski." He started walking up the aisle toward the main entrance. He knew she was listening to him.

"There are many, many evil people in Cape Noire. Most frequent the dens and alleys of Old Town. Do your hunting there and do no harm to the innocent. That is all I ask. Or else I will have no choice but to come after you."

With that Brother Bones exited the floor of the stadium. A few minutes later, the hunched figure in the big hat and heavy overcoat moved out of the alcove sticking to the shadows and disappeared along another corridor.

💀 💀 💀

"Where is she?" Bobby Crandall demanded when he came running down the flight of stairs that opened into the stadium's main entrance lobby. Brother Bones, sans jacket and hat, looking like a beat up giant rag doll stood there awaiting him. "Where's Paula."

"She's gone."

"What the hell does that mean?"

"It means we...I was too late to save her."

The words penetrated the confusion in Crandall's mind. He looked at the corridor leading towards the main hall, then back at Bones, refusing to accept his pronouncement. The finality they conveyed was too horrific for him to suffer.

"I don't believe you."

Bones took hold of his arms. "The girl was bitten. She is one of them, now."

Crandall cried out, shook himself loose and suddenly struck out, hitting Bones in the face. The mask took the brunt of the blow.

"Enough!" barked the Undead Avenger. "What happens next is not up to us, Bobby Crandall."

Without another word, Brother Bones turned and walked through the front glass doors. Bobby Crandall watched him go, looked back at the long empty corridor, and felt something inside him moan in pain. Head lowered, he followed after his master and whatever damnation awaited them both.

EPILOGUE

The good-looking brunette with the long shiny hair strolled along the sidewalks of Old Town long after the midnight hour. She passed several prostitutes who gave her jealous, wary glances, afraid she was another lost soul who was looking to set up her own operation. But the young woman ignored them, even when they verbally insulted her with lewd remarks. They were not her prey.

Turning a darkened corner, she was suddenly grabbed by a pair of dirty hands and pulled into a small, tight alley and shoved against a brick wall.

A thin, drugged-up bum shoved a switchblade up before her eyes and said, "One peep out of you and I'll cut up that pretty face."

"What are you going to do to me?" Paula Wozcheski asked demurely, wondering if her acting was any good.

"Well," explained the filthy smelling mugger, "I'm going to take that purse off of you for one thing. And then, because you're so pretty, I think we're gonna have some fun."

He leaned his pitted, pock-marked face closer to hers, touching her cheek with his blade. "How do you like that,heh, little bird?"

"Actually, not at all," she replied. She could feel the new hunger building up inside her like a demanding tide about to crest. She could smell the man's blood through the veins in his neck and she knew it was time to feed.

She reached up, took hold of his wrist and snapped it like a twig. Before the man could register the pain and scream, she opened her mouth to allow her fangs freedom, then sought his jugular. She tore into it, stifling his scream forever.

As she drank his warm blood, he dropped the switchblade. Paula would use it when she was finished to remove his head. She would not be responsible for turning any others. No, Cape Noire would have only one vampire. One who would heed the words of Brother Bones.

THE END

THE PLASTIC ARMY

Chad Jones pulled up to the Baker St. bus stop, downshifting his long green and red bus to glide her into an easy halt. It was shortly after midnight, and the streets of Cape Noire were almost deserted. His passengers at this time of the night were hotel service people and shop clerks going home after an exhausting day of work. Most were familiar faces that politely gave him a nod or even mumbled a few words of greeting.

Jones loved driving the night shift as he didn't care for the hustle and bustle of the city during daylight hours. Cape Noire was a major port city here in the northwest and, according to the last census, home to twelve million people. Just the thought of that many people coming and going on these old and narrow streets give Jones anxiety. No sir, he preferred empty streets with still emptier bus stops.

As a pair of cleaning women came out of the small sheltered sidewalk station, Jones observed a man standing statue-like at the end of the corner. At first he didn't pay him any mind. But as the two women took the steps into his vehicle, their arthritic joints unable to move them faster than a pregnant turtle, the driver gave the strange pedestrian added scrutiny.

With the dim glow of the streetlamp, the man appeared to be wearing a dark business suit, a fedora, and carrying a small briefcase. What bothered Jones was the fellow's skin color looked pasty, like bottled glue. But that could simply be a trick of the light washing down on the man and deceiving Jones' eyes. He pulled off his eyeglasses and wiped them with the handkerchief he kept in his jacket breast pocket. It was summer in Cape Noire, but being on the coast the night temperatures had a way of falling into cooler zones like this evening.

With both women now settled into their seats a few rows behind him, the bus driver closed the accordion doors, popped the clutch and started his big metal carriage forward. The light at the corner had turned green just as he pulled away from the curb and he gave the engine a little more gas to make the crossing.

For a second he forgot about the man on the corner until he suddenly walked right out onto the road and into the bus.

Chad Jones screamed, the impact vibrating through the blunt front end of the bus. He was pushing down on the brake pedal so hard, his heart beating at triple time. All the warnings by his wife Gladys about his being overweight and not going in for a checkup where echoing within his chaotic thoughts. He had just run over a man!

Ten years on the job without ever a fender-bender and now he had killed someone. As the bus' gears ground to a halt, he shut off the engine and sat back gulping air.

"Dear God, Jonesy," one of the two women said behind him crossing herself, "what did you do?"

He looked back at her unable to answer. It was the dumbest question he'd ever been asked.

Then he was opening the door and all but flying down the steps. To hell with the heart attack, what if the poor guy was still alive? He had to find out.

Coming around the front of the bus, he was scared silly at what he would find; some kind of pulpy mess of what had once been a human being.

He was not expecting to see an arm and leg torn from the corpse both a good ten feet away from the rest of the body. He moved closer to the squashed figure lost half under his giant steel bumper and bile rose up in his throat. He guy had been flattened like a pancake.

But where was the blood? Shouldn't there have been lots more blood… and gore splattered everywhere?

Jones moved closer cautiously, the scene before him becoming stranger by the second. The body didn't look so much like it had been smashed as it had been broken. As he came within a foot of what he could see of the torso, he began to make out the head; the hat having been knocked off during the impact.

The head was on backwards and the face, what was left of it, was looking up at him. One half had collapsed inward like a deflated balloon but there was nothing inside. No bones, no brain matter, no muscles torn apart. It was an empty shell of a head.

Now mystified beyond imagining, Jones went down on one knee beside the remains and reached out to grab the ruined face. The remaining half broke away in his hands and he screamed for a second time.

His mind was in total confusion as he brought the cold, inanimate piece up to his face and realized what it was he was holding.

"Plastic?"

"Heh," he heard one of the woman ask behind him. They had followed him out of the bus, their own morbid curiosity getting the best of them.

Chad Jones twisted his body around and held up the artificial face in his hands.

"It's plastic!" he declared. "It's not a real person."

"Hmm," retorted the nearest old woman. "Then how the hell did it up and walk in front of the bus?"

Jones mouth fell open.

How indeed?

☻ ☻ ☻

The black and white patrol moved through the dirty streets of Old Town like a hunter on the prowl for unsuspecting prey. Inside the sedan, Sgt. Wayne Bradford rode shotgun while his partner of six years, Officer Dane Canary sat behind the wheel. Both of them were bored beyond words and eager to wrap up their route through the worst district in Cape Noire.

"Hey, look over there," Canary pointed to where the car's headlights were sliding over the gray warehouse facades leading to Chancy Avenue and several bars frequented by foreign sailors. The twin yellow orbs had captured a young woman standing by a front stoop, smoking a cigarette. "Looks like we got a new working girl in the neighborhood."

"Hey, let's stop and give her a neighborly welcome," the grizzled sergeant said, his mouth clamped around a fat, cheap cigar.

The squad car came to a stop and the girl began to move away from the cement steps. She was dressed in pumps with stiletto heels, fishnet stockings and a tight black skirt that only reached mid-thigh. A loose, sleeveless red silk blouse was purposely unbuttoned to show a generous amount of cleavage with a white scarf tied around her neck completing the classic hooker image; selling hot sex to whoever had the ready cash. But it was her face, framed by mustard-yellow hair that caught Sgt. Bradford's attention as he quickly climbed out of the car.

"Hold it right there, honey!" he barked, fitting his cap on his blocky head.

The girl stopped and faced him. She remained silent, her round face with its rouged cheeks and bright red lips appeared both slutty and vulnerable.

"How old are you?"

"What's it to you?"

Bradford took hold of his leather gun belt with his thumbs and laughed, his pot-belly jiggling up and down. "We got us a feisty one, Canary. Real piss and vinegar."

The girl took a step back and saw that the other cop, this one taller and more muscular, had come up to the sidewalk to block her retreat.

"Who's your pimp?" Bradford pulled the cigar out of his mouth and pointed it at the girl. "And don't back talk me or I'll kick your teeth in."

Her blue eyes narrowing, the young prostitute saw no reason to lie. "I don't have a pimp. I just got into town a few days ago."

"Geez, fresh off the Hicksville express," Canary chuckled as he reached out a hand to touch the girl's yellow hair. At his touch she moved away. "Looks like she needs to learn the way we do things here in the Cape, heh, Sarge?"

"Officer Canary is right," Bradford continued, his phony smile still plastered over his rough-hewn face. "All you working girls need to have a handler, someone to look after you to see you don't get into no trouble."

Canary moved another step closer to the now scared teen. "Or else how are we to get our cut. Ain't that right, Sarge?"

"Cut?" The girl looked from one man to the other and the light of understanding dawned on her features. Slipping her small hand bag off her shoulders, she unsnapped it and began to reach in. "I get it. How much do you want?"

Bradford's small black eyes shone with the glint from the streetlamps as he saw the girl produce a wad of greenbacks tied together with a rubber band. She'd obviously been a busy girl for having been in town so short a time. Then again, he wasn't totally surprised by her financial success. It was easy to imagine regular johns in the area would have appreciated some new, fresh meat on the street.

"Jesus, Mary, Joseph, how much you got there, sweety?"

"About three hundred dollars."

"Then fork over two hundred and we'll consider this week's rent all paid up."

"What? You're crazy…"

Sgt. Bradford slapped her across the face with the back of his right hand sending her reeling back into Officer Canary. She cried out, the blow catching her by surprise and splitting her lower lip.

"Time you started showing some respect, missy," Bradford tossed his cigar into the gutter by the curb. "This is our city and if you are gonna come around selling your goods, you are gonna play by our rules.

"Do I make myself clear enough, deary?"

The girl wiped the blood off her lip and then tossed Bradford the wad of bills. "Take it. All of it. I don't care anymore. Just let me get out of here."

"Hey, what's the rush?" Canary leered as he wrapped his arms around the young prostitute and began fondling her breasts through her thin blouse. "Me and the Sarge here were hoping to sample the goods."

"No!" Frantically the girl tried to break free of the policeman's grasp only to have him rip the front of her blouse exposing one ripe breast.

Sgt. Bradford had caught the roll of bills and was happily removing the rubber band to count them for himself at the same time enjoying Canary's assault on the naïve young hooker. Oh, yes, he thought, this was going to be a good night after all.

"Let her go."

Both men looked around to the ink-black entrance to a small alleyway. A form had emerged and was approaching them like a shark cutting through water. The owner of the cold voice was a woman, average height, wearing a gray trench-coat, leather-calf boots and hatless. She had long jet-black hair and her face was classically beautiful with an ivory white pallor, high cheekbones and razor sharp eyebrows over cat-like green eyes that seemed to radiate in the darkness around her.

"Now who the hell are you?' The Sergeant stuffed the girl's money into his breast shirt pocket with one hand while the other fell on his holster which contained his .38 caliber revolver.

"I told you to let her go," the raven haired stranger spoke calmly as she continued to approach, her hands still in her long-coat pockets. "I will not say it again."

"Oh, really?' Sgt.Bradford pulled his pistol free, nodding at Canary to do the same. "It looks like we have ourselves a nosy troublemaker here."

Canary shoved the girl in his arms away so that she fell back into the parked cruiser as he turned and started to draw his own revolver.

He never finished the motion. The black haired intruder moved in on him so fast she appeared like a blur. Hands with long fingers suddenly materialized and took hold of Canary's shirt and then he was airborne, flying up and over his black and white.

He had time to give out a hoarse yell before he landed on his back, his head slamming into the road with a loud smack. His eyes rolled in their sockets and he passed out.

Bradford, reacting as fast as he could manage, leveled his gun and fired it straight into the mysterious woman. She took a half step back as the bullet punched through her, ripping out her back. But she did not fall. Instead she regained her balance and lunged for the fat cop. His mouth opened in stunned surprise as her hands clamped about his fleshy neck and he was yanked up off his feet.

He tried to bring his gun around only to have her swat it away with her left hand, maintaining her hold of him with only the right. The nails on her hand began lengthening and dug into his skin producing tiny rivulets of blood.

"Aaagh…what…are…?"

"What am I?" The brunette looked up at him and he saw her incisors as she spoke, they had become sharp and pointed. "I am all your nightmares come to life, you fat pig. I devour stupid creatures like you and your kind.

"And I am hungry tonight."

"Aghh…please…"

He could see the woman's eyes shining as she licked her lower lip then she looked over at the young blonde who had moved off the car and was trying to compose herself while watching the exchange between her tormentor and would be savior.

"Are you alright?" the brunette asked.

"I'll live," the girl answered, still unsure of what was happening. "Are you going to kill them?"

Paula Wozcheski, the vampire, looked back at the now weeping cop and shook her head. "No, not tonight." With that she flung the heavy man into the air sending him smashing into the building behind them. He hit with a thud and dropped to the sidewalk with another, where he lay moaning in pain. Paula hoped he'd broken something in the fall.

She brushed her hands together, hating to have soiled them with the filth of corrupt men. The blonde girl took a step onto the sidewalk and faced her.

"Are you a vampire?"

"Yes, I am."

"What's going to happen now?"

Paula could see the tiny smear of blood on the girl's lips and her own devilish needs swelled up inside her. She forced them to subside.

"What is your name?"

"Nancy…Nancy Hansen."

"Are you hungry, Nancy?"

The blonde's blue eyes took on a puzzled expression not sure what the dark bloodsucker meant by her question.

"There's a diner two blocks away," Paula added at the same time allowing a smile to appear. "They have great coffee."

"In that case, yes, I am hungry."

"Then let's go."

"Hold on a second." Nancy Hansen moved past the taller woman and going to the still groaning Sgt.Bradford bent down and rolled him onto his back. His face was badly scratched and bruised. She dug into his shirt pocket, retrieved her money and stuffed it back into her own purse.

Straightening up, she looked at the vampire and nodded. "Okay, lead the way."

☠ ☠ ☠

Night watchman Clancy Wilkins heard the siren screeching down the street past McLaren's Five and Dime and came awake in his little office in the big retail store's basement. A quick glance at the clock over his spindly desk indicated it was a half hour after midnight. He stifled a yawn and stretched his arms over his head. It was time he made another round of the two floors that made up the fancy downtown store. There was a sip of tepid coffee left in his plastic cup, and he drained it as he stood getting out of his padded chair on wheels. He grabbed his uniform cap off the table, adjusted his gun-belt, and picked up the heavy duty flashlight by his telephone.

Wilkins, a retired veteran, had taken the nighttime job to supplement his pension from the government. After all, these were hard times and though it was only him and his wife, Mildred now, they were getting on in years and her medical issues had drained most of their emergency funds. A proud man, Clancy Wilkins wasn't about to end up on the street like a lot of his former mates or, worse yet, go on the dole and allow the state to take care of him as if he were a pauper. His father had taught him at an early age that as long as a man could get out of bed in the morning, he was able to work. And there was no work a good man would shun to maintain his self-worth and integrity.

Still, shambling up the steps to the main floor, he had to ponder the vagaries of fate that had led a former leader of men to this menial job of safeguarding fancy merchandise for the city's elite.

He routinely walked the entire space of both floors every hour starting with the first floor and then taking the main elevator to the second and finally the back stairs up to the main offices where the clerks and accountants worked.

The three man janitor crew worked between nine and twelve every night leaving him alone until the day shift managers arrived promptly at six a.m. the next day. At first, Wilkins had found the job tedious and boring, but after a few months he began to enjoy the quiet and solitude.

As he moved through the sporting goods section, he waved the beam of his flashlight over the display cases where all manner of equipment and gear was stored on neatly arranged shelves and against the back walls where several plastic mannequins were attired in outdoor gear. The lifelike dolls always unnerved him with their cheery smiles frozen on their painted faces, their unseeing eyes staring into nowhere.

It was with these thoughts he realized something was wrong. Taking a step back to walk where the hunting scene had been staged, he realized the two mannequins he had seen there during his earlier pass were gone. But that didn't make any sense. Could he have been wrong about seeing them in his earlier circuit? Tilting his cap back with his free hand, he scratched the spot over his left ear. Maybe at sixty-eight he was starting to get senile after all. Standing there, he began to turn in a circle while slowly playing his light over racks and counters wondering if the mannequins were standing in a different spot and his memory had been faulty. Not a welcome thought, but one that would allay his rising anxiety, for he was sure he'd seen the two artificial figures; each dressed in boots, baggy pants, flannel shirts and hunting vests with shiny new rifles in their unfeeling hands.

There was a footfall behind him and Clancy Wilkins spun around.

"Who's there?" He shone his light past the shelves to the wider main aisle.

Again he heard noises. Feet shuffling.

The cautious night guard pulled his .45 automatic from its holster and, holding it pointed forward, walked towards the sound.

"If anyone is in here, show yourselves now!" No reply. "I've got a gun and I won't hesitate to shoot."

Entering the main aisle he turned to his left, the torch's spotlight illuminating a group of people. Wilkins jumped, a yelp escaping his lips. He hadn't been expecting to see that many people openly walking towards him in the dark.

It didn't make any sense.

"Who are you people?"

He held his light steady and could make out both men and women of various ages, but oddly all of the exact same height body structure. Then his light caught their unmoving faces as they marched closer and the realized they were not people!

They were mannequins! All of them; men attired in fancy sports jackets and slacks, while the women were decked out in the latest fashions, with gloves, handbags, chick hats atop their plastic heads.

"Stop…right there!" Wilkins ordered, his mind reeling as he did his best to hold on to his sanity. "What the hell is going on here?"

But the group of lifeless human replicas could not answer, their lips forever sealed in an eternal, horrible frozen smile.

Wilkins took several steps backwards. He had to run. To get help.

He turned around and was suddenly face to face with the two missing sports dummies. The closest stared at him with its painted eyes and then clubbed him across the head with the barrel of the rifle in its hands.

Wilkins cried out and fell to his knees, the pistol falling from his grasp. He looked up at the mannequins just as the second one leaned down and brought the stock of its carbine into his face, cracking his skull.

☗ ☗ ☗

Nancy Hansen couldn't believe how hungry she was until after she'd devoured the meat-loaf special followed by a huge chunk of cherry pie along with two tall glasses of milk. All the while, the vampire sat across from her in the diner booth, smoking a cigarette and drinking a cup of coffee.

The place was long, with a half dozen booths to either side of the main entrance and a counter fronted by red-topped padded stools. It was also practically deserted at this time of the night. A weary couple was seated in a booth at the opposite end of the diner and from their looks, Hansen figured them to be strung out on hash or some other illegal drug. An old man who appeared to have slept in his wrinkled brown suit was the only occupant at the counter keeping the one waitress, a plump, jolly soul named Honey, occupied with friendly banter.

The diner was open all night long with three short order cooks working revolving eight hour shifts. Ever since becoming a street-walker, the young blonde had come to know night owls of this variety all too well.

"When's the last time you had a decent meal?" the tall brunette creature said removing her cigarette from her painted lips.

"I don't really remember." The girl grabbed a napkin and wiped her mouth before taking another drink of milk. "I guess a few days ago."

"Where are you from, Nancy?"

"San Francisco," the girl was surprised the woman remembered her name.

"Why did you leave?"

"Look, I don't like playing twenty questions. How 'bout you answer some for me?"

The sexy bloodsucker grinned. "That's fair enough. What do you want to know?"

"What's your name...or do you even have one?"

"Paula Wozcheski. Though, I guess you're right. I'm really not her anymore."

"What does that mean?"

"Becoming one of the undead changes things. The world is different to me now." With that the vampire crushed out her cigarette and took another out of the pack by her now empty coffee cup.

"I thought vampires only drank blood?" Hansen knew she should be afraid but her curiosity was getting the best of her. Of all the things that had transpired in your young life, none was weirder than this encounter with a female vampire.

"You know, so did I," Paula Wozcheski concurred snapping a light from her Zippo and flaming the tip of her new smoke. She took a drag. "It's strange really. I still want to drink coffee, smoke, do all the normal things I use to do before I turned.

"You see, it really hasn't been that long."

"How did you become a vampire? Did someone else bite you on the neck?"

"Yes," the green-eyed woman said unconsciously touching the side of her throat when replying. "He was from Europe posing as a boxer. He told me he was five hundred years old."

"What happened to him?"

"He ran into something even more deadly than he was. It destroyed him while trying to rescue me."

"Oh, so why didn't this ...other thing ..."

"Destroy me too?"

"Yeah."

"I really don't know. I guess Bones felt sorry for what happened to me."

"Bones? As in Brother Bones?"

"Yes, the Undead Avenger of Cape Noire. You've heard of him, have you?"

"Uh-huh, but I really thought it was just a fairy tale. You know, like the boogie man and all that stuff."

Paula Wozcheski remembered the grim ivory white mask and shivered ever so slightly. "Oh, he's real alright. Pray you never encounter him, my dear."

At that moment, Honey materialized before them holding the glass pot of coffee. "Need a refill?" she asked.

"Yes, please," the vampire slid her cup over.

As she poured the hot black brew the waitress inquired if they wanted anything else.

When the brunette said, "No, that will be all," she put down the pot, pulled a bill pad from her apron pocket and ripped off the top page and slapped it on the table. With that she took up the carafe and disappeared.

"So," the blonde continued once they were alone again. "Why did you just save me now? Are you going to make me a vampire like you?"

"Would you want that?"

Piercing green eyes bore into nervous blue orbs. "I don't know. Life pretty much stinks anyway."

"Have no fear, Nancy, I did not save you from those uniform thugs to make a meal out of you."

"Well, that's good to know. But why did you help me back there?"

"Because since becoming a vampire I've realized I need a companion. Someone to guard over me during the day when I'm vulnerable."

"You want me to come live with you?"

"Yes, in exchange I can give you a clean place to stay, see that you never want for anything from now on."

"And all I have to do is watch over you while you're...what, sleeping?"

"Yes. Some of the old myths are true; like my not being able to go out into the sun. I have to sleep during the day and can only go out after dark."

Hansen pushed her empty glass away from her and avoided looking at her host. "Is that when you...ah..."

"The word is hunt, my dear. And yes, that is when the hunger for blood possesses me. But it's not all about that."

"Oh?" The girl looked up. "What else?"

"Believe it or not, I have a job and I plan on keeping it."

"You do?"

"I work at the Gray Owl Casino as a cigarette girl."

At that the blonde chuckled. "You're kidding, right?"

"No, I'm not. It's a decent job and I want to keep it if at all possible. I'm hoping you'll help me do that."

Nancy Hansen nibbled on her lower lipstick smeared lip. It was a lot to take in all at once. Still, no matter how bizarre it all was, it was still no worse than where her life was going now. The incident with the two cops had been proven that, despite her own inner toughness, she was an innocent girl alone on the streets of a hellhole like Cape Noire. Now this friendly vampire was offering her another option; one that might offer her refuge and time to heal her own damaged psyche.

"Alright, Paula Wozz…"

"Paula is fine, Nancy."

"I'll do it. You've got yourself a roommate."

"Excellent." Wozcheski's cold white hand reached out and touched Hansen's. "Where are you staying now?"

"A flop-house just around the block from here."

"Do you have anything there you need to pick up?"

"An old suitcase with some clothes and stuff."

"Then let's go get it and then I'll show you your new home."

As both women slid out of the booth, the brunette dug out several bills and tossed them on the table next to the bill.

Coming out of the diner, they heard several loud sirens in the distance. Both of them looked up trying to discern from where the wailing was originating.

The vampire, whose senses were heightened beyond normal human limits, tilted her head slightly and said, "Something is going on uptown."

"Is it always so noisy here?" Hansen asked as they started down the sidewalk side by side.

Paula Wozcheski grinned. "Dear, this IS a quiet night in Cape Noire."

Ambulance driver Fred Styles pulled his white vehicle around the corner almost on two wheels and spotted the accident scene ahead to the left of the boulevard. There was a black and white radio patrol car parked diagonally in front of a city bus and he could see the two cops talking with the driver by the curb. He killed the siren blaring on the roof of his emergency vehicle and, crossing the road, he parked alongside the bus in the middle of the street.

"We're here," he notified Pete Samerset, his partner in the back.

As Styles jumped out of the front seat, Samerset pushed open the rear double doors and came barreling out. Styles, a thin man with gray hair and glasses, dashed around the bus to confront the officers. Samerset busied himself pulling out a canvas stretcher for picking up the victim.

Having been a driver for St. Mary's Hospital for over ten years, he was familiar with most of the flatfoots in the city and Officer Stanley Burnham was no exception.

"Yo, Burnham, where's the pedestrian who got hit?" Even as the words came out of his mouth, he turned his gaze downward and saw the remains still spread out on the road half under the long fender. "Holy smokes!"

"Hold on," the copper said raising his right hand. He left the driver and his partner and hurried over to white jacketed men. "It's only a dummy."

Styles looked down at the body mumbling, "What the hell has his I.Q. got to do with anything?"

"No," the annoyed officer repeated, pointing down at the mangled figure at their feet. "It's not a real person. It's one of them store dummies they dress up in window displays."

Styles blinked. Samerset was standing beside him holding up the folded stretcher ready to move. Tilting his hat back on his head, the professinal driver crouched down beside what looked like a man in a natty business suit and saw that it was a mannequin, half its head missing and hollow.

"Sonuvabitch," he groused getting up again and confronting the cop. "Is this some kind of a sick joke?"

"Damn if I know, Fred. We took the call just like you. Then when we got here this is what we found. Driver says the thing walked out into the street just as he was pulling away from his stop."

"Huh? How does a dummy walk?" Styles looked over Burnham's shoulder at the excited bus driver who was still jawing away at the other cop; Burnham's partner Jeff Hayes. Beside the bus' few passengers, other curiosity seekers had begun to assemble on the sidewalk to watch the show. Obviously insomnia was big in this part of the city.

Styles made a drinking motion with his hands as if tilting a bottle to his mouth and Burnham nodded.

"That's what I thought too, but he's sober as a judge. And the folks on the bus all corroborate his story."

"IT'S ONE OF THEM STORE DUMMIES THEY DRESS UP IN WINDOW DISPLAYS."

Styles turned to his associate and indicated the ambulance. "Whatever is going on here, it's not our concern as there's no body."

"Lucky you," Officer Burnham commented. "Wait till I have to tell the Watch Commander about this one. He's gonna have my hide."

Samarset was sliding the stretcher back into the hospital van when there was a explosive crash and the front window of Gaylord's Mercantile shattered across the street. Everyone was startled, several of the women screamed. For a second no one moved, all eyes fixed on the ruined plate glass now covering the sidewalk and part of the street before them.

Officer Burnham moved around Styles and his partner to get a better view of the ruined store front. "What the hell...?"

A man appeared from inside the store and carefully walked out through the windowless gap. He was followed by a second man and then a woman.

"Are you folks alright?" Burnham called out but none of them responded. They merely continued to walk towards him in an awkward mechanical manner. And more were appearing from within the store; all men and women walking in the same exact lockstep.

As they moved out onto the street, trampling over the millions of shards of broken glass, their true identity became evident in the dim light of the streetlamps.

They were all mannequins!

Officer Burnham backed away rapidly from the walking dolls just as another store front window a block down the street exploded outwards. Two seconds later, a third did the same thing at Douseau's House of Style on the corner just beyond the accident site.

This one began to disgorge female mannequins walking stiffly in high heel shoes, wearing only the latest in Parisian fashions.

The cop, having rejoined his partner and the others in front of the parked bus, watched in disbelief as each group of shambling faux-people began to circle them, coming together in utter silence save for the sounds of their feet stamping down on the road.

"What are they doing?" Fred Styles got into Burnham's face. "What are they doing?"

"How the hell should I know," the unnerved peace officer retorted angrily, his face reddening.

"They're like them dead people come back to life," one of the old ladies remarked, clutching her heavy handbag against her body like a shield. "You know, like in that movie, *White Zombie* with Bela Lugosi."

Styles kept looking from one group to the other, wondering if he was having a nightmare and praying he'd wake up soon.

"They're surrounding us," Officer Jeff Hayes offered and everyone turned to him as if he'd just discovered the secret to the universe. "Look," he added for emphasis, pointing down the street behind them to the third group now massing together and marching up the middle of the street while the group from the lady's shop was completely integrated with those plastic-faced things that had walked out of Gaylord's.

"God, how many are there?" bus driver Chad Jones asked as the people around him began to move tighter together.

Officer Hayes had been right; the living mannequins were circling them, moving forward at a methodical rate, coming closer and closer with each passing second.

Officer Burnham suddenly pushed through the people around him and dashed for his patrol car. He knew this would bring him closer to the eerie dolls, but he had to get to his radio and call for help. He had parked it across the center of the street.

As he reached the driver's side he was met by a half dozen mannequins blocking his path. He drew his service revolver and aimed it at them.

"Get out of my way, or I'll shoot!"

But they were just inanimate things and not one showed any reaction to his words. They merely continued to come at him. He fired and his bullet tore a hole in the female dummy nearest to him, ripped out her backside and into the plastic statue behind her. Other than the hole, the bullet had no affect on them and they kept coming.

Then they were pushing him back against the front of the patrol car, their artificial bodies making it impossible for him to move. Burnham tried to shoot again, but one of the things pushed his gun arm down while another wrapped its stiff hands around his throat.

He tried to scream but his voice was cut off.

Two more shots rang out as Officer Hayes charged into fray. He'd seen Burnham's failed attempt to stop the creatures and didn't believe his own rounds would have any better results but he couldn't simply stand by and let his partner go down without trying to do something. Deep in his heart, the young cop thought it was the end. Neither of them was going to survive this night of madness.

💀 💀 💀

The crowd on the sidewalk watched in horror as the two cops were overwhelmed, each of them frozen with fear.

Suddenly, a pair of twin yellow lights flowed around the nearby corner and everyone turned to see a small, dark gray roadster appear going faster than was practical. Its tires screeched as the driver fought to bring it around and then it was barreling right up the middle of the street straight at the largest group of mannequins.

The car was moving so fast, none of the walking dolls were even aware of its presence until its front end plowed right through them. Plastic bodies were flung everywhere into the air, their artificial bodies torn apart with severed arms and legs being sent flying in all directions. Those not sent ricocheting fell under the racing automobile, its front grill smashing several of them at the same time its four tires bounced over the bodies of others.

It was like a motorized bowling ball crashing through a row of moving candlepins and when it was free of them it had left a pile of destruction behind it.

The people watching were totally mesmerized by their sudden salvation. The car roared to the end of the boulevard where it made a sharp U-turn and came racing back for a second run.

Meanwhile, the two officers were taking advantage the car's effective attack on the mannequin army by managing to fight their way free of those holding them. Burnham had taken the worst beating and had suffered multiple cuts on his face and hands. He was breathing heavily as Hayes helped him move away from their cruiser.

Seeing them break free, Styles and several others rushed to help them.

Then the roadster appeared past the parked police car, rolled around it and stopped with a hard jolt. Before any of the battling mannequins could look to see what was happening, the passenger door of the mystery car popped open and from it emerged a tall, menacing figure draped in a heavy black overcoat and matching slouch hat that hid half of his face. In his hands were two silver plated .45 automatics and without hesitation, he opened fire on the remaining murderous dolls. The grim marksman used customized bullets and each of his shots pulverized the plastic heads they hit, leaving the mannequins to stumble and then collapse.

The shooter laughed, raising his head and his bone-white skull mask was exposed for all to see.

"It's Brother Bones!" Fred Styles mouthed.

Ignoring the citizens he was saving, the Undead Avenger of Cape

Noire left the roadster and marched into the remaining plastic fiends, his twin guns continuing to blast away, spits of flame shooting from their hot barrels.

All the while, no one paid any attention to the freckle-faced young man behind the wheel of the roadster. Blackjack Bobby Crandall was as shaken by what he was seeing as the other people on the sidewalk. When Bones had ordered him to drive through the crowd assembled in the middle of street, Crandall had thought he was being told to run over living souls. Then, when his roadster had impacted with the mannequins, his surprise had left him stunned and speechless. Once again the Undead Avenger that was his boss had pulled him into another weird adventure unlike anything he'd ever seen before. Still, he'd managed to keep control of his car and bring it around for another pass as he was directed. Now, he watched as Brother Bones moved through the remaining plastic killers like a scythe through wheat.

It was all over in minutes. Nearly sixty mannequins had been ripped asunder, their parts scattered all over the street from one end to the other.

Brother Bones, his guns smoking, stood looking about to ascertain he had vanquished all of the soul-less replicas. Satisfied, he spun about, marched back to the roadster, climbed into the passenger and closed the door behind him.

His cold black eyes looked at Crandall through his ivory skull mask displaying no emotions whatsoever. The Undead Avenger was as stoic as the things he had just demolished.

"We are done here," he said. "Drive."

Gulping, Crandall nodded, pulled the stick shift into reverse and backed up the small automobile. Its rear tires bumped over dummy parts. He twisted the wheel back towards the way they had come, shifted into first gear and pumped the gas pedal.

Brother Bones rolled off into the night as quickly as he had appeared.

Detective Lt. Dan Rains climbed out of his unmarked police car and took in the circus-like activity in front of McLaren's Five & Dime. Wooden saw-horses had been used to close off the entire area in front of McCalren's and the other two shops from which the moving mannequins had appeared. Four black and white patrol cars were also clustered together and uniformed officers were helping keep the large crowd of people away from the parked ambulance.

It was a little after six in the morning and Rains was still fighting off the last touches of sleep. The call from the Police Commissioner had jarred him awake and he wasn't still certain of everything his boss had related to him in their all-too-brief ten minute conversation.

From the gist of what he'd been able to retain, while washing and dressing hurriedly, was that plastic store dummies had somehow come to life in the middle of night and gone on a rampage in the swank commercial district. Driving across town to the scene, he'd received a radio call from headquarters informing him the McClaren's manager, upon arrival at the store, had discovered the body of the night watchman amidst overturned shelves and scattered merchandise within the store itself. He had apparently been bludgeoned to death.

Walking past the patrol cars, he pulled the brim of his hat down to cover his eyes from the rising sun. He was both perplexed and annoyed as his shift didn't normally begin until eight. But then again, what was normal for a cop in Cape Noire, he mused. They had taught him in the academy that once he took up his bronze badge he would be on duty every minute of his life until which time he was either buried or retired. The odds were equal for both endings.

"Lt. Rains!" He recognized reporter Sally Paige's voice. She was pushing back several of the blues who weren't too happy about being assaulted by a dame, even one as pretty as the tenacious newshawk. "Please, how about a word for the morning edition?"

The uniformed boys looked at Rains and nodded. Better to deal with her quickly and then get on inside to find who was in charge of the investigation so far.

"Thanks," the Tribune reporter said, catching her breath as she hustled over to him. In her hands was a worn notepad and pencil. "So is it true, did a bunch of store front dolls come to life last night and kill someone out here?"

"Sally, right now you know as much as I do."

"Which is what, exactly?'

"Not a whole lot." He swept his arm around to indicate the city road crews who were in the process of picking up mannequin parts up and down the street. "I just arrived on the scene and it looks like one royal mess to me."

"What about the one that walked out in front of the city bus and started the whole thing?"

"Yeah, that." Rains did his best to recall the Commissioner's account.

"The driver is at the station filing a report while another man from the city garage picked up the bus and got it out of here so our boys could do their jobs collecting evidence."

"Is it true the cops who answered the call were attacked by those … things?"

"To some extent. Both were taken to St. Mary's and patched up. I really can't say anymore until I've had a chance to read their reports."

Paige was scribbling swiftly onto her notepad. "I also heard Brother Bones made a timely appearance. Can you confirm that for me?"

"No, I cannot. Look, that's about all…"

Just then, the front doors flew open and Fred Styles and Pete Samarset came out carrying a sheet-covered body on their stretcher. As they made their way to the open back of their ambulance, the crowd quieted down out of respect for the dead. They carefully slid their cargo into the back of the van then Samarset climbed in and pulled the doors closed.

Styles started around to the driver's door, saw Lt. Rains and touched the tip of his white cap in acknowledgement. Rains returned the nod.

The ambulance took off and the detective returned his attention to Miss Sally Paige.

"That's it, Sally."

"All for now, okay?"

"Hmm, okay. But you know I'm going to follow this up," she smiled mischievously.

"I never doubted it for a second." He leaned his head closer to hers. "If you stumble onto anything, anything at all…"

"I know the drill, Rains. You'll be the first to know."

"Thanks."

He stood watching her walk away admiring her slim figure and long, shapely legs. The two of them had been friends because their occupations brought them together often, but he'd always wondered if it could be something else. One of these days he was going to take a gamble and ask her out on a real date. Now that might prove interesting in all kinds of pleasurable ways.

Bringgg! A telephone started ringing in a booth at the corner to his right. It continued to do so until one of the men in the crowd went over and picked up the receiver. Rains watched him with mild interest. Who would be calling a public telephone at this hour of the morning? Especially when there would be no one around to answer it.

Shrugging, the seasoned investigator started to turn for the store's entrance only to be stopped by someone calling his name.

"Hey, are you Lt. Rains?" It was the fellow in the phone booth. He was leaning out holding the receiver in one hand and pointing it at Rains.

"Yeah?"

"It's for you. Some guy said he wants to talk to Lt.Rains."

Now that was strange, Rains thought, as he headed for the booth. The only people who knew he was there were his colleagues and they would have contacted him either by a radio call to one of the squad cars or a direct phone call to the store manager's office.

So who was using a public phone to tag him?

"Thanks," he said to the helpful citizen and taking the black receiver, replaced the fellow in the narrow confines of the glass and wooden booth.

He brought the phone to his ear. "Hello, who this?"

"Greetings, Detective." The gravely voice penetrated Rains' being and he was instantly alert.

"Brother Bones!"

"It is I. Listen carefully, when questioning the store manager, ask him about Mott Smalley."

"Why? Who's this Smalley and what's ..."

Click.

Lt. Rains pulled the phone from his ear. It was, like his eerie caller, now dead.

☻ ☻ ☻

Bobby Crandall came out of the bathroom drying his rust colored hair with a towel dressed only in his gray pants and barefoot. Looking up across the kitchen of his small two bedroom apartment, he saw Brother Bones turning from the telephone mounted to the wall. The grim masked avenger had removed his slouch hat so that his pure white skull mask was completely visible as was the top of his head covered by a mat of stiff, wheat-like bleached hair; hair that never grew.

Even after two years of living with Bones and performing his duties as his aide and chauffeur, young Crandall was still uncomfortable in the supernatural being's presence. Little things like Brother Bones' mask staying on without strings or any other attachments spooked the lad. As did the undead vigilante's cold black eyes.

"Get some sleep, Crandall," Bones directed. "This incident is far from over."

"I gathered as much," Crandall said draping the towel around his neck and going to the icebox set against the wall across the room. He opened it and grabbed a half gallon of milk which he brought to the stove and poured into a sauce pan. Warm milk always helped him fall asleep, especially after a night battling alongside Bones.

"I mean, mannequins coming to life and attacking people, what the hell is that all about and who's behind it?" He turned on the gas burner while pulling a porcelain cup off the pantry shelf above the stove.

"I don't know," Bones admitted as he removed his heavy topcoat. Beneath it he wore a leather shoulder rig which was affixed to twin holsters, one under each arm containing his silver plated Colts. "My spirit guide only pointed me to the store and then uttered a man's name. That is all I know."

The milk was beginning to boil. Crandall poured it into his cup and shut off the stove. "Okay, so what was the name?"

"Mott Smalley."

"Is that the person behind what happened out there?"

"I do not know. I just gave his name to Detective Rains. Perhaps he can learn more about this person for us."

"For us? Ha, that's a good one. Rains would as soon lock you up as he would Harry Beest or any other crook in Cape Noire."

"Regardless, he is a good man and thus worthy of my assistance when I can provide it."

"While at the same time you use him to get whatever information your will-of-the-wisp spirit guide forgets to pass along." Crandall took a sip of the warm milk. He really needed to sleep. His evening shift at the Gray Owl Casino started at six p.m.

"I do whatever is required of me," Brother Bones reiterated to his young assistant. "You know my existence continues only at the mercy of the fates. Only by punishing the wicked do I have any hope of atoning for my sins."

With that Bones grabbed his hat from the back of the chair where he had set it and opened the door to his bedroom.

Without turning he ended their conversation with a parting word. "Get some sleep, Crandall. I shall not disturb you."

Bobby Crandall sighed, his thoughts jumbled. Initially at the beginning he'd served the Undead Avenger out of pure fear. Brother Bones had saved him from a gangland execution and for that he had demanded servitude of the young card dealer. But after witnessing firsthand the bloody crusade Bones waged single-handedly against the many forces of evil to protect Cape Noire, Crandall had come to understand and ultimately support the black-clad warrior of the shadows. He was still afraid, but somehow the righteousness of Bones' mission had won him over.

Crandall had no idea where their partnership would take him, but two years later he was determined to see it through to whatever end awaited them.

He put away the milk and with his cup in hand entered his own darkened bedroom.

Maybe he would be blessed with pleasant dreams.

💀 💀 💀

"Gentlemen, I'm facing a crisis of epic proportions here," sweaty-faced Leo Gardner, Manager of McClaren's Five & Dime, declared to the two detectives sitting in front of his ornate desk in his office on the top floor of the giant department store.

"My second floor is still a mess, you've got the front of the store blocked by policemen and will not allow me to get a repair crew in to fix our front display window." The big man with the balding head and piggish small nose pulled a gold-plated pocket watch from his vest pocket and examined its ticking hands. "And we open in just under ninety minutes. This is a disaster."

"If you'll pardon me, Mr. Gardner," Lt. Dan Rains held up a hand to stop the fat man's tirade. "This is a crime scene and no one is allowed to contaminate it until our forensic people have examined it thoroughly to process any hard evidence."

Pushing his tiny, rimless glasses up from the tip of his nose, Gardner was clearly not delighted with that reaction. "That is totally unacceptable. Do you have any idea what kind of financial setback this will be? Not only for today but the foreseeable future. Our loyal customers will read about this horrible event in the papers and then be afraid to shop here. They'll lose their trust in McClaren's and…and…"

"You'll be getting a pink slip," Sgt. Sean Duffy finished. He was a small man with straight sand-colored hair sitting to Rains' left. Duffy was one of the few detectives the lieutenant respected and trusted; he was smart and straight as an arrow.

Hearing the words he dreaded, Gardner grabbed for the pitcher of water on his desk, filled a tall glass and gulped half of it before speaking again. "I've been employed here for twenty-five years, gentlemen. I am not about to give up my job without a cry for justice and reason. I happen to know the Mayor quite well; he and I play golf together quite often and…"

"Mr. Gardner," Rains interrupted. "Who is Mott Smalley?"

"What…Smalley. Why do you want to know about him?"

"I repeat, who is he?"

"Why, he was a former employee here. In fact he was the Display Designer for us going on two years." A glimmer appeared in Gardner's eyes. "Do you suspect him of being involved with what happened here last night?"

"One thing at a time," Rains didn't want to lose his focus. "You say he was in charge of displays. You mean he oversaw the placement of the store's mannequins, their clothing etc.?"

"Exactly. And he really was quite good at it, though he was queer as a three dollar bill."

"What do you mean?" Sgt. Duffy had found his own dog-eared notebook and was ready to start taking down whatever facts Gardner provided them. "Queer how?"

"Well, if you must know, Smalley was a pansy…ah…a mother's boy. From what I recall of his personal file, his father deserted them when he was only a child and he was brought up by his mother who doted on him endlessly. I mean, here was a grown man still living with his mother."

"Nothing wrong with being a loving son," the Irish cop countered, thinking of his own saintly mother living in the Heights.

"Oh, it was more than that, I assure you. Every time Smalley finished a new display arrangement in one our windows the old lady would come down on the bus to check it out. Honestly, she would come into the store and examine each piece of the diorama like some army inspector. The poor boy was a nervous wreck until she gave him her approval."

"You said former employee," Rains took over. "So he no longer works here?"

"No, we had to let him go…hmmm, let me think. Yes, about six months ago. Just at the start of the year."

"Why did you fire him?"

Gardner took another big drink of water. "Frankly, because he started acting peculiar." He saw Duffy tilt his fedora up and rushed to finish. "More so than usual. You see his mother died last year. It devastated the poor fellow. Naturally we gave him time off to handle the arrangements etc. Many of the girls who worked in his department went to the funeral. He was Jewish, I think.

"Anyways a few weeks after her passing, one of the girl's reported to the

Floor Manager that Smalley had started acting…ah…strange around one of the new dummies we'd just gotten in."

"How so?" Duffy looked up from his notepad.

"It was a female model and according to what I'm told, he began to… well, act inappropriate with it. He was caught fondling her." Gardner's face took on a sick expression. "One morning, one of the girl's came in early and found him embracing the thing. She was only dressed in underwear and Smalley was kissing her…it…you now what I mean!"

"So you canned him," Duffy concluded aloud.

"Well, not at first," Gardner said in his own defense. "He was given several warnings. One of our personnel people even suggested he see a psychiatrist. It was obvious his mother's death had unhinged him. But he refused. It was as if he didn't care. When the next complaint was filed we had no choice but to fire him.

"Believe me, we hated to do it."

"Alright," Dan Rains rose out of his chair and Duffy did the same. "We're going to need this Smalley's home address."

"My secretary should have it in her files."

"Thanks. You've been most helpful, Mr. Gardner. We'll see what we can do about speeding up the boys out front and getting out of your hair."

"That would be most appreciated, Detective."

As Rains and Duffy exited Gardner's office into a smaller reception area where the manager's secretary, a stout, middle aged woman, was seated behind a small desk to their right, Duffy leaned into Rains and whispered. "Where'd you get this tip on this Smalley character?"

"Let's just say an informant and leave it at that."

Rains turned to the receptionist to ask for Smalley's address hoping his friend wouldn't push it. Explaining their one lead had come from Brother Bones was not something he was ready to share.

Bright sunlight filtered through the lace curtains waking the man with the curly brown hair and sharp angular face. He stifled a final yawn with the back of his hand, pushed the sheets off his torso and stretched out his arms cat-like. Looking at the sunlight he smiled. It certainly was going to be another beautiful day in Cape Noire.

The door to the bedroom opened and the love of his life entered carrying a tray with his breakfast on it. He could smell the fresh bacon and the aroma of black coffee immediately. He twisted around, propped his pillows up against the backboard and pushed himself into a comfortable position.

The woman leaned over carefully as to not spill anything and put the tray down over his lower body. Her golden yellow hair fell down framing her angelic face as she did so and he gazed into her cold beauty. She'd smudged her ruby red lipstick a bit and that made him smile. Make-up application was a hard lesson to learn but she was diligent and always doing her best to please him.

"Thank you, Alice," he said looking at the plate of scrambled eggs, bacon with buttered toasts resting on a napkin beside the cup of coffee. Folded to the opposite side of the tray was a copy of the morning paper. He wondered if the news of the night's events had made it into this sunrise edition. He would have to find out; but first breakfast. He would read the paper with his second cup of coffee.

"Do sit, Alice and keep me company while I eat."

Alice took a step back and sat down in the blue padded chair by the lamp table. She was wearing furry slippers, frilly black panties with a matching bra and a see-through black negligee. As ever, she sat demurely with her legs together, her hands folded very lady-like on her lap as she watched him.

The man who had once called himself Mott Smalley sighed contentedly looking at Alice. Of all the mannequins he had ever known, she was the loveliest, her image cast in sheer feminine perfection; a perfection no flesh-bound woman could ever hope to equal.

Unlike the others he had brought to life, Alice responded faster to his instructions and, day by day, her movements gained greater fluidity. One day, she would be the most graceful woman in the world.

And she was his. Above all else, Alice was his and his alone.

Unable to resist any longer, he picked up a crispy brown strip of bacon and bit into it, enjoying its exquisite taste. He could never eat the forbidden food without hearing his now deceased mother loudly admonished him in the ways of their traditions. He could see her pointing her finger at him in a scolding fashion. "Be a good Jew, Mott. God is watching you all the time."

Then he would go to school and get the stuffing beat out of him by the cruel, gentile boys who had learned their anti-Semitism from their churchgoing mothers and fathers. As they punched and kicked him repeatedly, calling him vile disgusting names, he learned the true meaning of hypocrisy. The world was ruled by ignorant bigots and if you were not a member of the right political group, the correct faith, the proper skin color, then you were looked down upon as something less than human.

"Be a good Jew, Mott," his mother would say, dragging him to synagogue on the Sabbath. He never wanted to go, but the bullies had broken him and he didn't have the heart to fight anyone, including the old lady. So he went to temple, he took Hebrew lessons, and he studied the Torah, all without enthusiasm. It was all just more stupid things to learn as he grew up on the streets of Cape Noire; a bitter, lonely young man trapped in a sad and boring life.

Then, one day, Rabbi Horowitz told him a story about an old rabbi from the old country that, through diligent study of the sacred books, had brought a monster to life to protect the people of his congregation from their tormentors.

At first, Smalley had scoffed at the tale. It was childish fantasy told to scare children, like many of the stories from the Torah; all of them meant to keep Jewish boys and girls in line and obedient to the ways of their traditions. Still, there was something about that story that was different from all the others. This man-made monster actually set about destroying their enemies with a savage fury he completely approved of.

Oh, to be able to create such a thing and have it do his bidding; which was when Smalley had the idea of digging deeper into the old legends himself. What if they weren't just superstitious fairy tales? What if one could make a sculpt a monster from clay and bring it to life?

It took him almost a full year to learn the magic incantations from the ancient scrolls locked away in the basement of Temple David, the Jewish synagogue he attended. Access to these was restricted to only the most devout Talmudic scholars, and he had used every ounce of persuasion at his command to convince Rabbi Horowitz he was such a student. At first he couldn't believe his luck, but by the time he'd mastered the black magic spells, the realization of what he was going to attempt began to appear impossible.

He wasn't a sculptor, and procuring that much clay would certainly raise a few eyebrows; never mind that he had no place to work on such a construct. The small two-story house he and his mother had lived in was cramped from floor to ceiling. Frustrated, Smalley reluctantly gave up the idea.

Then, one day, while setting up a new diorama for McLaren's front window, he found himself looking at the plastic mannequins and wondering if maybe the ancient esoteric formulas might work just as well on them as they supposedly had on a giant clay effigy.

Maybe, just maybe, he could create something totally different along the same veins as the old legend.

Then, within weeks of having this epiphany, his mother did something truly wonderful for him.

She died.

☻ ☻ ☻

Wildwood was a small residential suburb located southeast of Cape Noire. It was mid-afternoon by the time Lt. Rains and Sgt. Duffy found 182 Elm Lane, the home address of Mott Smalley. It was a plain white cape house with a square green lawn and one car garage attached to right.

There were two little boys playing catch on the grass when Rains brought his unmarked sedan to stop.

"Didn't Gardner say this Smalley lived alone with his mother?" Duffy questioned as the two men climbed out of the car.

"Maybe we've got the wrong house?" Rains walked around the car looking at the mailbox post.

As luck would have it, a black mailman came walking up to them, his leather pouch weighing heavily on his left shoulder, several envelopes in his right hand.

"Howdy, gents," he said, opening the mail box and sliding the letters in. "You look lost. Can I help you?"

Rains and Duffy grinned and the lieutenant pulled out his badge while identifying himself. "You sure can. I'm Lt. Rains and this is Sgt. Duffy. We're looking for the Smalley residence."

"Well, you came to the right place," the postman confirmed. "But he don't live here anymore."

"Oh?"

"Yeah, he sold the place and moved out a few weeks after his mother passed away."

"That would have been about six months ago?" Duffy remembered.

"Right. It was kind of sad, his losing his mother and all. They were really nice folks and well-liked here in the neighborhood."

"Would you happen to know where he moved to?" Rains asked hopefully.

"Hmm, I can't say. When I found out about his moving, I reminded him to be sure and leave a forwarding address at the office. But I don't know if he ever did or not. They never got much mail, him and his Ma."

Rains was starting to think they were going to end up with squat.

"What kind of man was Smalley. I mean, personally."

The mailman scratched his chin, reflecting on his memories. "Well, like I said, he was okay. Kind of quiet and shy. Which was why I was happy when he came into all the money."

"Huh, what money?"

"From his mother. Guess she'd been buying them stocks and bonds things the banks sell most of her life. Old Mott, he didn't know nothing about that until after she died when he got a call from the bank."

"And he told you all this?" Duffy once again had his notepad out and was busy jotting down this new information.

"Oh, yeah. I happened to run into him the day he was heading to the bank. He was all excited. Said his mother had left him with a fortune."

"Can you believe that? The old woman left him a rich man."

☠ ☠ ☠

The day wore on and the citizens of Cape Noire went about their normal activities, both routine and unexpected, both legal and illegal. The city lived and breathed and minutes flew into hours until the sun, weary from it all, dove into the Pacific Ocean leaving behind darkling skies.

Night began her dance across the skyline.

In his darkened room, Brother Bones sat in his chair looking out the window as he did every day. He did not sleep, nor did he dream; ever. His black eyes looked out upon this city of sin and redemption as he awaited his next summoning.

When the tall, thin candle on the bureau behind him came to flaming life, he turned his head. A yellow flame licked at the wick and brought forth a glow that surrounded the space around it. Bones rose up out of the chair and approached the candle. Beside it on the bureau top was his porcelain skull mask. Here, in the blackness of his sanctum, he went without the mask, his true face naked but remaining unseen. There were no mirrors in the room to reflect the horror of it.

As always happened, the wisp of a face appeared in the flickering flame. It was the face a young girl he had murdered long ago. For whatever reason, the fates that controlled his existence had decreed she be his spirit guide. It was through her, Brother Bones received all of his missions.

"Mott Smalley has escaped," the delicate voice told him.

"You didn't tell me where to find him," Bones retorted, annoyed by a declaration that sounded too much like an accusation.

A YELLOW FLAME LICKED AT THE WICK AND BROUGHT FORTH A GLOW.

"I was not allowed," she continued. "I am only a messenger."

"So? What now?"

"He will strike again and more will die."

"How does he animate the dummies?"

"He has learned the secret of the Golem."

"The what? I don't understand. What's a …golem?"

"Dark magic born of perverted faith."

"I figured as much last night."

"Be wary, my avatar of final justice. Remember, magic, of any source, can destroy you."

The image began to dissolve in the fire.

"Wait. How? Where do I look?'

"Find and punish him."

The flame died out with a curl of gray smoke.

Brother Bones slammed his fists into the bureau and the candle fell over. He set the candle upright again and let the frustration he was feeling ebb. "Damn ghost, always speaking in riddles."

He picked up his white mask and carefully placed it over his decayed visage. The mask remained there without any strings or adhesives.

Twin black eyes looked through the slits.

What the hell was a Golem? Then he recalled the words the spirit had used to describe the forces he was facing; perverted faith. *Faith.*

Brother Bones knew a man of faith.

It was time to go hunting.

☠ ☠ ☠

Blackjack Bobby Crandall threw his short-waisted jacket to Ivy, the pretty blonde manning the coat-room as he walked into the main lobby of the Gray Owl Casino to begin a new night of dealing twenty-one. As ever, the large, high-ceilinged main room was as busy as an anthill with dealers setting up their tables, bartenders and waiters stocking the two long bars on opposite walls of the casino, and the Pit Bosses checking the cash window to ascertain everything was ready for when the doors opened to the public.

Though the casino hours began at seven nightly, the large crowds didn't arrive until after eleven when most of the dinner clubs and theaters were closed. One thing young Crandall had learned early on was that gambling was a sport for late owls, ergo the place's name.

Stepping down the two steps to the green-carpeted floor, he looked across the crowded room and spotted the elevator doors opening. All accounting operations and the manager's office were located on the second floor. It was who he saw coming out of that elevator that stopped him mid-step as if someone had just punched him in the chest.

Tall, statuesque, with her jet-black hair reaching down to her naked white shoulders, Paula Wozcheski moved through the hall, skirting the various gaming stations dressed in her high heels, fishnet stockings and a one piece black bathing suit; a white choker and wrist cuffs completed her outfit.

Crandall immediately moved to intercept her, waving off his own boss, Sal Havers, who was over by his own table talking to one of the casino waiters.

"In a minute, Sal," he yelled, keeping his eyes on the woman. When she heard his voice, she looked at him and then started to walk off in another direction to avoid him.

Crandall raced around the roulette wheel quickly and cut her off just as she was passing the hallway that led to the restrooms.

"Paula, stop!" He grabbed her left elbow and positioned himself in front of her. "What the hell are you doing here?"

It had been three weeks since he'd last seen her. She had failed to report to work. He'd called her flat a dozen times only to hear the bell ringing endlessly. In desperation, he had even gone to her place and banged on the door. But no one had answered, and eventually several of the other residents had made their displeasure known by his presence. The building super had threatened to call the cops unless he left.

So here they were, three weeks later and she was standing before him like nothing had happened out of the ordinary, to include her absence from the club.

"I thought you would have figured that out," she answered, "after what happened."

She was, of course, referring to the incident with the Bavarian vampire.

Crandall was at a loss for words. He'd been so worried about Paula for so long, his imagination running wild with ludicrous, awful scenarios and now that she was in front of him, he didn't know what to say next.

"Look, Bobby, I just talked Mr. Russell into not firing me. Now I've got to get back to work if I want to keep my job."

"Just like that?" He was more confused than ever. "Paula, what … happened to you?"

She leaned in closer lowering her voice. "I thought your friend would have told you that."

Other employees were beginning to take note of their conversation. "Come on, we can't talk here." He started to grab her elbow again, but she pulled it back.

"We've got nothing to talk about, Bobby."

"Baby, please. I went nuts worrying about you. At least talk to me. It will only take a minute." He nodded his head towards the cloak room.

Looking at the curious faces around them, the brunette sighed and acquiesced. Together they walked across the floor and past the Ivy's counter into the tight room where a dozen steel bars hung suspended from the ceiling and were festooned with hundreds of plastic coat hangers.

Moving to the furthest corner of the empty room, Crandall tried again to get her to talk. "Bones told me you'd been…bitten. That you're a vampire."

"He told you the truth, Bobby." She folded her hands over her bosom in a defiant posture. "That's what I am now."

"But there must be something we can do to reverse…ah…this?"

"No, there isn't. The only thing that will end my curse is death. Real death. And you know what I mean."

He ran a hand through his red hair becoming more frantic. "No, I won't believe that."

Wozcheski opened her arms and put a hand on his shoulder. "Bobby, we have to accept this and move on."

He looked into her green eyes wanting to find some spark of the affection they shared.

"Without each other," she finished. "Whatever we had is done. I'm sorry, but it has to be that way."

"NO! I can't accept that."

"Then you're a fool. Good-bye, Bobby."

She started to walk away and he again tried to restrain her. The vampire spun around, grabbed him by the throat and lifted him off his feet. Her face became something menacing and when she opened her mouth, he could see her pointed fans.

"I kill people and drink their blood," she hissed. "Do you understand me? DO YOU?"

Crandall was gasping, her grip on his throat cutting off his air. "I… don't…care. I…love…"

She let him go and he fell to the floor landing on his right hip. He coughed, trying to catch his breath. He looked up in time to see her walking out of the room. She never looked back.

☻ ☻ ☻

After finishing vespers, evening prayers, old Father Dennis O'Malley rose up from the communion rail as fast as his arthritic knees would allow him. The pastor of St. Michael's Catholic Church started down the aisle of the empty church anxious to lock the front doors, put out the lights, and retire to the adjacent rectory where Mrs. Callaghan, his cook and housekeeper, had a pot of beef stew on the stove.

The only lights still on were those behind him high over the beautiful marble altar where he conducted daily mass and officiated over other church rituals. Thus the back of the immense knave was lost in a black gloom. Still, having been the pastor of St. Michael's for over twenty years, the old priest had no problems navigating his way to the front vestibule and the two giant oak doors.

He was coming up to the last rows of pews when a movement in the gloom caught his attention and startled him.

"Sorry, padre," a deep voice apologized. "I didn't want to scare you."

"Saints alive," O'Malley gasped, putting a wrinkled hand over his heart. "Then you shouldn't be sitting all by your lonesome way back here in the dark, sir."

The figure sitting on the wooden bench remained silent. O'Malley's old eyes behind his rimless bifocals couldn't make out anything clearer than a bulky lump.

"Why don't you come nearer so I can see you, sir. My eyes aren't what they used to be. I'm afraid."

Brother Bones stood and walked out of the shadows.

Seeing his ominous figure, the large slouch hat, heavy overcoat and the frozen white mask had the cleric making the sign of the cross while taking a full step back.

"Lands sakes alive, what are you?"

"Men call me Brother Bones, padre. Do not be afraid, I'm not here to hurt you."

O'Malley studied the grim avenger whom he had read about often in the newspapers. This was his first time seeing the person, if that's what it truly was, up close. Then his memory kicked in and another strange encounter from his past resurfaced in his mind.

Touching a bony index finger to his lips, he spoke to his mysterious visitor. "Two years ago I had another big man visit me in the night. He was a killer named Tommy Bonello and he came to me seeking salvation."

"Yes," Bones said without feeling. "You sent him to a place of peace and prayer."

O'Malley nodded and, moving back, sat down on one of the pews and waved at the space beside him. "Later that place was destroyed by more evil men, like the man I'd tried to help."

"It was not your fault." Bones sat beside the old priest and removed his hat. "Evil was not finished with me. I had to die first." Without his hat, the white skull mask seemed even more chilling, the dead eyes visible through the twin holes.

Once again Father O'Malley crossed himself. Although he'd never come face to fa,ce with Brother Bones, on several occasions in the past two years he had assisted through the avenger's intermediate, a young fellow with freckles on his face.

"I often wondered if you and Mr. Bonello were one and the same."

"It makes no difference now, padre. Tommy Bonello is dead and what you see before you is…something else."

"Well, I know from what I read that you are no devil, sir, and that you are most certainly on the side of the angels. What is it I can do for you, Brother Bones?"

"Have you ever heard of something called a Golem?"

O'Malley blinked. "A Golem! My boy, if you are searching after a golem, you've come to the wrong church."

"What do you mean?"

"Only that the Golem is an old Jewish legend. You'd be better served talking with Rabbi Horowitz at Temple David, the synagogue across town."

"Sorry, padre, but I have no time for that. Can you help me or not?"

"Well, I can tell you what little I know."

"Then do so. I have a madman to find and stop."

O'Malley wished he was back in his quarters. He'd have poured himself a stiff shot of whiskey before proceeding, and he even considered inviting the macabre specter to join him there. Then he remembered Mrs. Callaghan and nixed that idea immediately. The drink would have to wait.

"Well, as I recall the story…ah…legend takes place in Prague during the Middle Ages and involves a very powerful rabbi named Loew. It was said he was knowledgeable about all kinds of ancient spells written down in the old Jewish scrolls. Amongst these was one particular spell that would allow him to breathe life into a giant figure made of clay, thus mimicking God's creation of Adam and Eve."

"Why would he want to make such a monster?"

"Because at the time his people were being persecuted by the authorities because of their faith. Not a new story amongst God's Chosen Ones. Loew built the Golem, that's what the thing was called, to destroy their oppressors."

"Does the legend say how he did this? How he made it come to life?"

"Well, there are several versions," O'Malley continued. "The most popular one is that Loew, after chanting the spell, wrote the word *emet* on its forehead; *emet* meaning *truth* in Hebrew. Then, when he wanted to stop it, he wiped off a single letter changing it to *met* which translates into *death*."

Brother Bones was silent for a minute, letting what he'd learned filter through his own experiences with the animated mannequins. Finally, he asked, "And how does the story end, padre?"

"Like all dark fairy tales," O'Malley confessed. "After the Golem had destroyed Loew's enemies, he lost control of it and it went on a rampage throughout the city destroying everyone who crossed its path, both guilty and innocent.

"Loew finally managed to hunt it down and destroy it. He left the city in shame and was never heard of again."

Bones stood up and put his hat on, tugging it snug over his head.

"Thank you, padre," he said moving past the old pastor.

"Wait," O'Malley turned around in his seat. "Is there such a Golem here in Cape Noire...now?"

By the tall front doors, the Undead Avenger looked back and nodded. "Yes, but not just one. So long."

Then he was gone and the priest was alone in the church. Looking to the altar and the crucifix suspended above it, he bowed his head and clasped his hands in prayer, fear gripping his heart.

"Sweet Jesus, I don't know what creatures you've set him against, but please, be with him on this night." He crossed himself a third time.

☠ ☠ ☠

Detective Lt. Dan Rains sat back in his swivel chair and stretched out his arms to get the kinks out of his back. The small clock on the wall behind him indicated eight p.m., and through the single window to the right of his desk he could see the city draped in its night lights.

His tie undone, sleeves rolled up to his elbows, Rains could feel the strain of the long day starting to wear him down. He picked up the half-empty coffee mug on the desk and took a sip; too late realizing it had gone cold whereas the tasteless pastrami sandwich he'd wolfed down for dinner was letting him know he was in for another bout of indigestion.

He looked at the ruined plastic head resting by the phone to his left, and wondered for the hundredth time what it was he had missed. Before him on the table, under the harsh light of his desk lamp were scattered reports turned in by all the officers and witnesses connected with the "living dolls" incident. That's what the Cape Noire Tribune had declared the matter in a three inch font over its evening edition; the byline credited to Miss. Sally Paige.

Rains had read what the cops had documented about the mannequins coming to life, about the timely intervention of Brother Bones and store manager Leo Garnder's statements regarding one Mott Smalley. Just as he'd guessed earlier after their fruitless drive to Wildwood, he and Sgt. Duffy had been unable to find a forwarding address on Smalley. He'd simply taken his mother's inheritance and vanished.

Rains wasn't even sure Smalley was a genuine person of interest. They had no hard evidence the fellow was involved with the matter; only a lead from an undead vigilante.

The tired investigator reached into his shirt pocket and pulled out a pack of cigarettes and lit one up. As he blew out the wooden match and dropped it into a glass ashtray, he looked at the broken dummy's head and marveled at how lifelike it had been shaped and painted.

Which was when his muse struck and he snapped his fingers. Clamping the smoke tight in his lips, he leaned forward and pulled the giant city directory from under his black telephone and quickly began to flip through its hundreds of pages.

There was a soft knock on his door. Without looking up, he said, "Yeah, come on in." Out of the corner of his eye he saw Sean Duffy's light brown hair as his partner entered the small office.

"You planning on spending the night?" the Irish detective asked.

"Hold on a second, Duff," Rains had found the page he was looking for and reached for his phone. He pulled it to his ear, heard the operator's voice, and gave her the number he wanted. Then he took one last drag on his smoke and crushed it out in the ashtray.

Duffy sat on the desk's corner and folded his arms across his chest, curious as to who his boss was calling.

"Hello, Mr. Gardner," Rains acknowledging he'd reached his party. "This is Detective Rains. Yes, I know it's late and I apologize for disturbing you like this, but I need one additional piece of information from you."

Rains paused and then nodded his head. "Yes, sir. What I need to know is where do you get your mannequins from? Is it somewhere local or out of town?"

Duffy leaned over, pulled a pencil from Rains' desk caddy and handed it to him. Rains ripped out the top page of his tiny desk calendar and began to write on the back of it. "Yes, sir, I've got that. Yes, sir. Thank you. Good-bye."

Rains dropped the phone on its cradle and began looking through the directory again.

"What was that all about?" Duffy inquired. "You got some kind of lead?"

"Not really," Rains replied as he found the page he was looking for. Once again, he wrote something on the small slip of paper.

He pushed his chair back and stood up and started to roll down his sleeves before going to grab his jacket and hat off the clothes rack behind his desk. "Just an idea I'd like to follow up on. Want to go for a ride?"

"Where to?"

"Cresthaven Park."

Sgt. Duffy was familiar with the small community located north of the city on the coast road. "What's up there?"

"Chandler Wax Works," Rains provided as he finished putting on his coat and started for the door. "That's where they make those store mannequins used in McLaren's and most of the other shops here in town."

Minutes later both men exited from the side door to Police Central and climbed into an unmarked Ford sedan. As they drove out of the parking lot into the street, neither spotted the tall, grim figure that stepped out of the alley across the street and watched them drive off with dead black eyes.

The white sliver of a crescent moon hung low in the cloudless night sky over the woods surrounding the Chandler Wax Works factory. The giant warehouse had been built several miles from the heart of the rural hamlet known as Cresthaven. On entering the village, Rains and Duffy had stopped at a two-pump gas station to top of the car's tank after the hour-long drive. There the attendant gave them easy directions to the plant and told them because it employed a second night shift, they would find it in full operation when they arrived.

They turned off the main drag onto a dirt road and passed the fence surrounded Shiloh Bottling company to their right. The place was dark and quiet. Next to the locked up front entrance was a huge painted billboard announcing, NOW THE HOME OF WYLD ALE with the picture of a muscular lumberjack hoisting a giant mug of frosty beer.

"I'd heard about this place being turned into a brewery," Duffy commented as they drove by. "Wonder what the stuff tastes like?"

"I'll buy you one once we wrap this up," Rains promised keeping his eyes on the road ahead. They drove another quarter mile before coming to a large, rectangular building and stopped in the parking lot. Getting out of the car, Rains counted twenty other vehicles in the lot and thought business must be good to maintain two production shifts. Lights peeked out from the building's many windows and loud machine noises were heard as the two detectives headed for the front door. To the far right of the structure, they could see the extension of what had to be a loading dock and beyond it were several packed hauling trucks.

Rains went up the four cement steps, opened the front steel door, and entered, Sgt. Duffy right behind him. There was a small corridor which led them to an open door and through it into the huge cavernous main floor of the wax-works.

Here they found three massive vats ten feet high filled with hot, bubbling pink wax. The vapors rising from the heated material produced a sweet, cloying smell. Dozens of tubes located at the bottom of the vats were connected with dozens of molds being operated by men wearing thick leather gloves, aprons and surgical masks tied about their faces. The two officers watched as several of the employees raised the top halves of their casting molds, revealing the finished parts within. Some conveyor lines were for arms and legs, while the workers stationed behind the other vats were pulling out torsos of various genders. The end of the last belt was surrounded with rolling racks on which were loaded hundreds of bald, pink heads.

As they walked into the area, Rains could see the factory's length was that of a football field, and beyond the casting area he could see long benches where several women were putting the various doll parts together and then standing them up on round wooden bases with the aid of a steel rod. He watched as the finished mannequins were dragged to both sides of the building by the rear exit doors. He estimated there were at least a hundred of them all ready for shipping.

A pudgy fellow in bib-dungarees and a red bandana tied around his neck approached them holding a clipboard in his hands. He had bushy brown hair and wore thick glasses.

"Gentlemen, can I help you?"

Rains flashed his police badge in his wallet folder. "I'm Lt. Rains and this is Sgt. Duffy. We're with the Cape Noire police looking for some information regarding a crime that took place there last evening."

"Oh, I see."

"And you are?"

"Curtis Maloney," the man extended a calloused hand and Rains shook it. "I'm the foreman here. So, what do you need to know, Lieutenant?"

"We were informed that the mannequins made here are the ones purchased by the big retail stores in the Cape. Is that right?"

"Yes, it is. But if you want to talk about that, maybe you should talk to the boss himself."

"You mean Mr. Chandler is here now?" Rains thought their luck was finally changing.

Maloney shook his head. "Well, no. You see, old man Chandler ain't the boss anymore. He sold the company a few months back."

Rains and Duffy exchanged glances. "So who is the owner now?"

"That would be Mr. Biggers. Mort Biggers." Maloney turned around and pointed to the far back wall behind the giant vats. "After he bought the company, he had some of the empty offices up on the second floor remodeled into an apartment and moved in. There's an elevator back there that will take you up."

"I see," Rains could see the lift doors. "What's he like, the owner?"

"Mr. Biggers? He's a good enough guy, I suppose. He's fair to the employees, gave us a quarter raise when he took over the place, and has increased production to almost double what it was before.

"You want I should give him a call and let him know you fellahs are here?"

"Sure, why don't you do that."

"Hang on, I'll be right back."

Rains and Duffy watched the foreman walk off to a work table bolted to the wall to their immediate left. There was a phone and intercom box on it.

Duffy moved closer to Rains and whispered. "Mort Biggers. Are you kidding me?"

"I know, I had the same thought. If its Smalley, he's got a twisted sense of humor."

They could see Maloney talking with someone on the phone, he looked at them and smiled and then hung up. He signaled them to follow him.

"Mr. Biggers said you should come on up," Maloney said as he led them around the furthest vat and down the aisle between it and the outer wall. At the end they came to the gray elevator doors. There was only one button on it. Maloney tapped it and the doors slid open.

"There you go," he said backing away.

"Thanks for your help," Rains said and entered the private conveyance with Sgt. Duffy.

The doors slid close, there was a tiny jar and then they were moving upwards. Neither said a word, each waiting to see what awaited them.

The elevator stopped, the doors receded and a lovely young woman, with golden hair, wearing a pale blue dress stood before them, her arms comfortably at her sides.

Lt. Rains took a step forward, a smile on his face until he saw her plastic face. He stopped, his hand instinctively moving to his hip where his .38 caliber revolver rested in its holster under his coat.

The lady doll bowed slightly, turned and swept her left arm out towards the apartment behind her.

Sgt. Duffy gasped and then muttered, "What the hell?"

The mannequin walked away from the two startled detectives into a spacious penthouse living room designed in rich Art Deco décor. Everything wad done in a black and white motif with a plush white rug on the floor, black leather sofas facing each other over a glass and silver coffee table and a fully stocked bar at the other end of the ornate room. Three walls were covered with modern paintings, each under a tiny light and there were marble statues located throughout the room.

In the middle of this ostentatious decoration stood a man of average height with curly brown hair and pencil thin mustache. He was wearing spats, pin-striped gray pants, a matching vest and dark blue shirt open at the collar.

"Ah, officers, welcome to my humble abode," he smiled, opening his arms wide to greet them. "I am Mort Biggers, the owner of this company."

Rains and Duffy approached him walking side by side, each wary after encountering the animated mannequin. She had walked to Biggers' side and stood facing him.

"Can I offer you both a drink?" He tilted his head to the blonde doll.

"My lovely Alice here mixes a wickedly delicious dry martini."

"This isn't a social call," Rains explained showing off his badge again. "And I'm thinking you already know why we're here, Mr. Biggers."

"Suit yourselves," Biggers turned to Alice. "One dry martini, my dear."

The mannequin nodded and walked over to the bar to make the desired cocktail. As she did so, Biggers clapped his hands together and addressed his visitors.

"And yes, Lt. Rains, I am well aware of why you are here. Frankly, I'm surprised it took you this long to find me."

"Cut the crap," Sgt. Duffy spoke up, becoming annoyed with the man's lackadaisical attitude. "You're Mott Smalley, aren't you?"

"There's no point in denying it, is there? But Mott Smalley was the old me. The weak, pathetic fellow who had no backbone and let the world shove him around all the time. But no longer, gentlemen. You see before you a new man, one reborn with greater potential to do amazing things."

"Like bringing wax dolls to life and having them go on a killing spree?" Rains was keeping one eye on Alice, still unnerved by her very presence. It was one thing to have read the reports about what others had witnessed but an altogether different experience seeing it with his own eyes.

"Alas, there were scores to settle. Leo Gardner is an insensitive pig who treated me horribly all the years I worked for him. And he never gave me one word of praise or encouragement. Not one." The color was rising in Smalley's cheeks at the memory of those tortured days. "Then, when my mother died he never bothered to attend to funeral or even send me a card of condolences. No, instead he continued to be his old obnoxious self until he found an excuse to fire me. Frankly, that was the biggest favor he ever did me."

The blonde Alice had finished making his drink and, as he ended his tirade, she stepped up to her creator and handed him his drink in a small cocktail glass.

"Thank you, my dear," Smalley touched her cheek with his free hand as he took the mixed drink and gave it a sip. "Ah, perfection as always."

"Okay, enough with the hearts and flowers," Duffy interrupted. Like Rains, he was nervous near the articulating mannequin woman. "Just how the hell do you do it? Bring them to life like this?"

"Why, magic of course," Smalley answered freely. "An arcane spell taught to me by a rabbi all about a monster called the Golem."

"The what?"

"Golem. Long ago in ancient times a rabbi brought a giant clay figure to life by inscribing a word on its forehead and then reciting a magic spell." Smalley turned to the mannequin. "Alice brush back your hair, please." Then he motioned for the two detectives to step closer and see for themselves.

At first Rains saw only the smooth plastic outer shell but then as he peered harder, he made out a very clear, transparent word that was as vague as a watermark on fancy stationary. But he still couldn't make out what it was.

"I can barely see it. What does it say?"

"It's stamped in Hebrew, Lieutenant. The word is *emet*. It means *truth*."

"Well, here's a truth for you," Sgt. Duffy pulled a pair of handcuffs out of his pocket. "You're under arrest, Smalley, for murder and multiple counts of attempted homicide. Put your hands out."

Mott Smalley looked at the steel bracelets and then sighed. He finished his drink with a gulp and handed the glass back to his Alice. "Clean this and put it away my dear. Then remain here until I return."

The finely sculptured Alice returned to the bar with the empty glass and Smalley put out his hands. "Very, well, let's get this over with it."

Duffy snapped on the cuffs, then, taking Smalley's elbow, guided him out of the room and towards the elevator. Lt. Rains watched the mannequin called Alice wiping the empty martini glass behind the bar, not even looking at them. In his career, Rains had dealt with lots of weird cases; this one being one of the more unusual. The sooner they had Mott Smalley safely behind bars back at Police Central, the better he would feel.

Duffy had already hit the button and there was a tiny ping as the doors rolled open for them.

☠ ☠ ☠

As soon as they began to descend, Smalley bowed his head slightly and began to mutter strange words neither officer could understand.

"What are you doing?" Duffy slapped Smalley's arms roughly.

"Why, I'm just praying," their prisoner replied. "You have something against a man praying, Sergeant?"

A befuddled Sean Duffy looked at his boss confused. Lt. Rains merely gave him a shrug as if to say it was beyond his own rationale. Duffy scratched his temple and returned his stare frontward choosing to ignore Smalley.

Mott Smalley grinned, bowed his head once more and continued his strange utterances.

The elevator stopped, the doors disappeared and the trio walked out into the middle of the factory. The wax vats were to their right, the tail-end of the assembly lines to their left. They started down the center aisle; the two detectives keeping the handcuffed Smalley between them. Several of the night-shift workers watched with curious glances, each wondering what was going on with their employer.

All the while Smalley kept mouthing his incantations.

Foreman Maloney was conferring with a grease-covered belt-mechanic when he spotted them. He came rushing over, wiping his hands on the bandana he'd been wearing around his neck. "Hey, what's going on guys? Why you got the boss cuffed ..."

Just then they heard a woman scream.

Dan Rains turned to his left and saw several women backing away from the assembly area. The assembled, nude mannequins were jerking about on their stands, arms and legs flailing about like giant theater puppets. Suddenly, one managed to free itself from the support rod and stepped off its pad onto the cement floor. Another repeated the trick and within seconds several others had followed suit. Then the marching mannequins raised their arms and began moving towards the frightened women.

All of the girls abandoned their stations in terror as more and more of the dummies became animated and joined the others. The unattended conveyor belt began pilling up plastic arms and legs at its end cowling until they began to spill over onto the floor.

In all the confusion, Maloney started to go towards the machine controls only to have Rains pull him back. The detective had his gun in his hands as did Sgt. Duffy.

"Get your people out of here!" Rains commanded.

"But the machines...?"

"Screw the machines...you want to die?"

"Rains!" Duffy pointed past them. One of the fleeing female workers had tripped and fallen to the floor, knocking down the woman behind her. They were directly in the path of the oncoming dummies.

Sgt. Duffy charged forward, pistol held out before him. He fired two quick shots; one hit the closest mannequin in the chest blowing a hole through it, the other missed completely.

"Move it, Maloney!" Lt. Rains repeated. "Get everyone out. NOW!"

The loud retort of the gunshots had alerted all the other workers and everyone was looking about the floor trying to find its source. Maloney took off running around the various production lines yelling at his people to shut off their machines and flee the building. Rains watched him for a half second satisfied he was following his instructions.

He turned to Smalley. The man was still mouthing the strange Hebraic phrases, and Rains knew it was how he was animating the lifeless plastic effigies.

He put his .38 right in Smalley's face. "Stop it ...NOW!"

To his stunned amazement, Mott Smalley looked up at him with his glazed-looking eyes and then shook his head negatively. He was daring Rains to stop him. The detective thumbed back the hammer on his revolver, holding it steady and pointed at the spot between Smalley's cruel eyes. But the man continued his speak his evil spells.

More shots rang out and Rains spun around. Looking past the escaping workers, Rains saw that Duffy had managed to pull both fallen women to their feet and pushed them along. He'd then stood his ground to protect their retreat and was firing point blank into the silent creatures that surrounded him. His bullets ripped off chunks of plastic bodies but did nothing to halt the mannequins in the slightest.

One of them swung its arm out to strike Duffy and he ducked to avoid the blow only to have another come in from his side and kick him in the legs. Losing his balance, the tough cop fell over, his hat knocked from his head. The mannequins closed in around him, all punching and kicking.

Forgetting Smalley, Dan Rains bolted down the aisle screaming, "Get off him, you freaking ghouls!" But his words had no effect as the mannequins continued to pummel his partner. Almost on them, Rains opened fire, hitting several of the bare backs forming a wall around Duffy. All this did was tear pieces off the dolls.

Frustrated, he holstered his pistol and began pulling the mannequins off Duffy. He would grab them from around their cold plastic necks and yank them backwards off their feet. Managing to pull two off, he started on a third when one of the dummies on the floor suddenly rose up on one knee and tackled him from behind. Just like that he was lying beside Duffy on the hard floor.

"Thanks...for...the help," Duffy managed to offer, his hands up covering his now battered face.

"We've got to get up," Rains said stating the obvious.

"Yeah..." the bloodied sergeant chuckled. "Piece of cake."

BOOM! BOOM! Two loud gun-blasts echoed throughout the factory and two of the savage mannequins' heads exploded above them. Rains twisted his body around and tried to look through the forest of plastic legs around him to see who it was that had come to their rescue.

BOOM! Another mannequin collapsed giving them a path to move through. As Rains managed to get to his feet, he leaned back, grabbed Duffy's arm and dragged him along.

Looking back towards Smalley, he saw a tall, grim specter materialize beside the occult conjurer decked out in his black greatcoat and slouch hat shading his grim bone-white skull mask; Brother Bones!

"Your death is upon you, Mott Smalley!" Bones declared, his voice carrying over everything, including the whining machines.

Smalley spun about and looked up into the visage that had judged him. He continued to speak his chants.

Brother Bones brought up one of his silver-plated .45 automatics and blew out the man's brains. Blood and gore sprayed out the back of his skull and Mott Smalley crumbled before the dark avenger.

At that very instant, all the mannequins ceased their movements and were still, frozen in place as if a giant puppeteer had released their strings.

Rains had Duffy on his feet and the two of them stood trying to regain their breaths, cautiously eying the mannequins as if they might suddenly come back to life. But they remained stationary; unmoving and unliving.

The two detectives joined Brother Bones as he stood over the remains of Mott Smalley, smoke curling from his two pistol barrels.

"It is done," Bones said looking at Rains, his black dead eyes revealing no emotions.

Rains began to respond when they heard a soft ping. The elevator against the back wall opened and from it emerged Alice, Smalley's personal mannequin. She walked stiffly to where they were gathered and, moving around Brother Bones, went to her knees beside the dead man. Then, very gently, she pulled his body up so that his bloodied head was cradled in her lap. She smoothed back his hair very carefully and then her head tilted to the side and she too was gone.

"How the hell...?" Rains looked from the female replica to Brother Bones. "How did she keep moving like that...after you'd killed him?"

Brother Bones put his guns back in his twin shoulder rigs beneath his heavy overcoat.

"Magic, Rains. Not the twisted, perverse magic Smalley sought to possess but the purest, greatest magic of them all; love."

By now, Curtis Maloney and some of the braver workers had dared to re-enter the facility and were starting to gather around them. Brother Bones turned on his heels and pushed his way through them making for the exit. At the sight of them, the men moved out of his way quickly.

Dan Rains, gun still in hand, thought for a split-second of stopping him, but realized his bullets would have no effect on the Undead Avenger. Bones had once again saved his life and Duffy's. Looking down at Mott Smalley and his Alice, Rains felt a deep sadness in his own soul. He heard the front door slam shut and knew Brother Bones was gone.

For now.

THE END

THE LADY
IN RED

There was a bright harvest moon painted across the dark blue night as Paula Wozcheski flew erratically over the port city of Cape Noire. The whole flying thing was new to her, only having become a vampire a few short months earlier from the bite of a Bavarian count posing as a prize fighter.

Initially, all she understood about her transformation were the things she remembered from old black and white horror movies; she lived off the blood of others, she was weak and vulnerable to the harsh glare of sunlight and, as a member of the undead, she possessed unbelievable strength and fantastical abilities. Of course, with no one to teach her what she was and was not capable of, things had pretty much relegated themselves to a tough course of on-the-job training.

During her life-altering adventure with the European vampire, she had watched him change into a giant, human-like bat and fly. Ergo, if he could do it, why couldn't she? For several nights, after her shift as a cigarette girl at the Gray Owl Casino ended, Paula had wandered into the darker alleys surrounding the club and there, away from prying eyes, had attempted to will herself to change. Nothing happened except her giving herself one throbbing headache after another. After weeks of failure, she began to believe such a transformation was beyond her. *Maybe only old, ancient vampires knew the trick*, she thought in frustration. Maybe she would never understand it?

Meanwhile her continual need for sustenance kept her roaming the streets during late night hours as she hunted for fresh blood. It wasn't always an easy task, as she had given her word to Brother Bones, the city's bizarre, creepy zombie-like protector, that she would never take the life of an innocent person. Per his clear directives, she only hunted the scum of the city, the lowlife criminals and thugs who preyed on the defenseless as Bones did. At first she had thought the idea ludicrous, but the more she acclimated herself to her new life as a blood hunter, the more she came to appreciate the fine line she walked between the light and the dark.

Somehow targeting only those who deserved her tearing fangs managed to assuage her own conscience and make her continued existence bearable.

Still, having to canvass block after block on her hunting forays had proven to be both physically tiring and time consuming. If only she could fly. Ironically, it was her new companion, Nancy Hansen, who had come up with the idea.

"Why not throw yourself off a building," the cute, ex-prostitute suggested one evening after she'd come home to the apartment they shared. Paula had rescued the girl from a life on the streets in return for her acting as the vampire's guardian during daylight hours. In the three weeks they had been together, the arrangement had become mutually satisfying for both of them. Paula was impressed at how easily her new friend had adapted to being roomies with one of the undead. Then again, having started turning tricks at the age of sixteen had given Miss Hansen a strong, resilient nature.

"That's crazy," Paula had replied without much thought. "I'd kill myself." Then she heard the words that had tumbled out of her mouth and saw the cat-like grin on Nancy's pretty face.

"Wait a second," she suddenly rationalized. "No I wouldn't, I'm…"

"A vampire," Nancy finished for her, chuckling.

They wasted no time in rushing out of their fifth floor rent and climbing the stairs to the eight and top floor of the building located in Old Town, a seedy part of the city. From there, it was up the final stairwell to the roof.

Once there, Paula walked to the stone balustrade and leaped onto it gracefully. Looking down she saw the sidewalk and nearly deserted street. It was almost 2 a.m. and, except for the occasional transit bus, there was no traffic or witnesses to see what she was about to attempt.

"Well, what are you waiting for?" Nancy asked, coming up behind her, munching on an apple she'd grabbed from the kitchen before they exited their flat. "If it doesn't work, you'll just get a few bumps and bruises."

"That's easy for you to say," Paula countered, her gaze still glued to the cement pavement below. "Even if it doesn't kill me, it's going to hurt like hell…"

"You're such a baby," Nancy lunged forward, stuffing the remainder of the apple in her mouth, reached out, and pushed the tall brunette off the stone railing.

Paula had screamed as she fell off the building, her body twisting in mid-air so that she was falling headfirst backwards. Her eyes looked up at the blonde girl in shock and instantly she knew she was about to become a big gob of splatter on the sidewalk.

And just like that she changed. In a matter of seconds, her entire body morphed, her arms grew longer and leathery wings appeared from them attached to her torso and thighs. Her knees became bony ridges and her feet became elongated with razor sharp claws just like those that her fingers had become.

She flapped her arms without any thought other than it was what she had to do and immediately her body swooped upward away from the street and she was flying. Her ears seemed to grow longer to pointed ends totally sensitive to the millions of sounds all about her and her eyes became black orbs that could see for miles in every direction. The sensation of soaring through the air was like nothing she had ever imagined before; it was both power and grace so elegantly combined that made her feel so alive. *Not bad for one of the undead,* she mused.

It only took her a few seconds to master the skill ,and then she turned in midair and returned to her building rooftop where Nancy Hansen was awaiting her.

Her landing was a bit clumsy and she almost fell on her face, her oversized, clawed feet were difficult to walk on. She steadied herself and stood facing her blonde companion.

"Wow, but that was totally something else," Nancy blurted.

"It was, wasn't it?" Paula's voice sounded strange coming from her distorted mouth, the elongated fangs garbling it somewhat.

"But I have to admit, you look really scary like that."

"Oh, right." Paula looked down at her leather-skinned monster body. "How do I turn back to...me?"

"I don't know," Nancy bit her lower lip in thought. "Maybe you should just think about yourself as you really are. You know, imagine it in your mind and make it happen."

Could it be that easy? Paula nodded, "Okay, I'll try." Afraid it might not work, she closed her eyes shut and began envisioning herself as she truly existed; tall, statuesque with long black hair and jade green eyes. She felt a sudden warmth spreading throughout her body, and when she opened her eyes, she was herself again.

And fully clothed. "That was weird," she admitted.

"What?" Nancy asked. "It worked. You're yourself again."

"I know, about my clothes? They vanished when I turned into the bat-thingee...and now...they're back again. I don't get it?"

Neither did Miss Hansen, though it became the main topic of conversation for the next few days. Eventually, both of them came to the same conclusion; that they were trying to solve a magical riddle using normal logic. Clearly in this case, normal logic, to include physics, simply didn't apply. To prove their theory, Paula went through the metamorphosis several times; only now she purposely dived off the roof rather than getting shoved by her friend. In every single instance her apparel simply went away as she became the human bat and reappeared when her normal body did.

Just something else to add to her new, extraordinary existence.

☠ ☠ ☠

All this past history swept through Paula Wozcheski's thoughts as she flew over the crowded tenement complexes located in a three block district of Cape Noire known as Little Jamaica west of Old Town. Just beyond these streets were the wharves of Crystal Cove and the waters of the mighty Pacific. Here, thousands of blacks and mulattos from the Caribbean Islands had relocated in hopes of finding a better life. Instead, what they discovered over time was that they had given up the poverty and squalor of their homeland for the cold, damp ghettos of the Northwest. The lesson to be learned; life was tough everywhere and only the strong survived.

Nearing the center of Little Jamaica, her sensitive hearing picked up angry voices; many male and one female. Zeroing in on the loud voices, she swooped down over one building and spotted the source of the clamor. Under a street lamp by a four way corner, several men were verbally threatening a young couple. Paula immediately dropped out of sight into a nearby alley where she transformed herself back into human form the instant her feet touched the ground.

She peered around the corner to better assess what was happening only twenty yards away under the glaring streetlamp. From what she was seeing and hearing, it wasn't difficult for her to realize she'd stumbled upon a highly charged racial incident about to get violent. Four black men, all of them appearing to be in their early twenties, were in the process of accosting a lovely young black woman and her white male companion. Apparently, the gallant fellow had dared escort his office co-worker back to her home despite the fact that Little Jamaica was predominantly a black neighborhood.

"You dare come into our streets!" the brashest of the locals was screaming at the girl's friend. "And putting your hands on one of our sistahs!"

"Stop it, Levon," the girl at the center of the altercation pushed back, as she purposely stepped between her white associate and the street gang. "Jerry is a co-worker who was kind enough to walk me home is all. He's got manners, not like you riff-raff."

"Hear that?" the one called Levon asked his mates. "Jalinda says we ain't got no manners. Maybe that's why she's dating a whitey, cause she's too good for her own kind."

Before the brave girl could say another word, Levon suddenly punched her in the stomach doubling her over. "Here's what we do with uppity bitches, sistah honey!"

To his credit, Jalinda's co-worker suddenly moved past her and knocked Levon on his his back with a solid right hook. "Leave her alone!"

And now it gets bad, Paula mentally predicted. She'd known people like Levon and his pals all her life. Having been the daughter of Polish immigrants, she had been bullied and made fun of during her own childhood because of her thickly accented English. Over the years she had learned to master her language, but she never ever forgot the humiliation she'd been made to suffer from those older, ignorant children.

So much so that she hated all forms of prejudice, either racial or ethnic. They were all the same brand of mindless cruelty, and now as these black punks were about to hurt someone for no other reason that his color was different from theirs.

She watched as Levon's buddies surrounded Jerry and all three attacked him at the same time, swinging their fists brutally until he collapsed and they continued their assault by kicking him. By now, Jalinda had regained her feet and was desperately trying to shove them away, but to no avail.

"That's it," Levon, back on his feet and wiping the blood off his upper lip said, urging his three companions to continue their savage beating.

Paula Wozcheski had seen enough. She stepped out of the alley and ran across the street moving in a blur. Then she was grabbing one punk by the back of the neck and throwing him out into the middle of the street. He flew well over twenty feet before landing on his back with a loud smack and didn't get up.

Levon and his pals were stunned at the white woman's sudden appearance. Then, when they saw her throw aside their friend so easily, their minds froze in disbelief.

"What th' hell…?" Levon started to mutter but he never finished his sentence. Paula moved around the bleeding figure of their victim, reached out, grabbed the other two assailants, and effortlessly lifted them both up by the throats so that their feet were kicking off the ground.

She slammed their heads together. There was a sickening crack as both were knocked senseless. She let them drop like lifeless bags of potatoes.

"SHEEIT!" Levon cried out before spinning around and dashing away down the street.

Paula turned to Jalinda and nodded down to the groaning Jerry. "Get him some medical help. Though I think he'll live."

"Ah...ah...yes, ma'am," the girl was clearly frightened of her.

Maybe she has a right to be.

She took off after the fleeing Levon. It was time to eat.

Levon Butterfield Jr. had the misfortune to run off into a dead end alley. He rushed past trashed cars overfilled with refuse, ran through scores of fat rats feasting on the waste humans discarded finally reaching the twelve-foot wire hurricane fence that blocked his end of the alley.

He could hear footsteps racing behind him, the click-clack of a woman's high heels. Huffing to catch his breath, he turned and faced the dark passageway he had just traversed looking for the scary dame that had physically vanquished his pals. He couldn't believe how easily she had tossed them all aside as if they were weak babies to be disrespected and unworthy of any extra thought.

Part of the shadows before him began to coalesce into an approaching figure. It was her, all black hair and tall, lithe body, moving towards him like a jungle cat without any hesitancy or fear whatsoever.

Levon reached back with his right hand to the concealed hand gun resting snug in his waistband under his dirty tee-shirt. He held up the snub-nose .38 with two hands and pointed it at her.

"Take one more step and I'll blow you away, bitch!"

The woman laughed. She actually laughed at him and continued coming closer.

"Have it your way!" He squeezed off a shot and saw her stop upon its impact. Thus he knew he'd hit her. But she didn't fall. And she just kept coming.

He fired another round and then another but they had no effect on her at all.

What the hell was she?

Paula, now within a few feet of her prey, casually slapped the useless gun out of his hands. She moved up to him so that he could clearly see her face in the light of the silver moon above. When she opened her mouth, her snow white fangs appeared.

As the vampire grabbed his shoulders immobilizing him, Levon cried out, wetting himself just before she bit into his neck and tore it to shreds greedily sucking up the arterial spray that splashed all over her lower face.

Paula Wozcheski drank him dry in five glorious minutes of feasting.

☠ ☠ ☠

It was close to three in the morning by the time Paula made it back home to the tenement building apartment she shared with Nancy Hansen. Flying low over the rooftops, she was surprised to see a black and white patrol car parked at the curb next to the front stairs and several cops standing there in conversation with the building's supervisor, Mr. Guler; a small man with thick glasses and wheat-colored hair.

Having a natural aversion to the police, she swiftly flew over them and landed smoothly on the roof before being seen. Transforming back to her human shape, she moved closer to the edge and listened as Guler thanked the officers for responding so quickly to his call. She wondered what was up but as long as it didn't concern her directly, it was best she ignored whatever it was.

Being Cape Noire's only resident vampire, drawing attention to herself was something she avoided adamantly. She opened the door to the stairwell and started down to the fifth floor and her rooms. When she came out into the hall, she was surprised to find Nancy, dressed in her bathrobe and slippers, talking with old Mrs. Breinmer whose hair was done up in rollers and her face lost beneath a ton of white beauty cream. Mrs. Breinmer lived across the hall and was, according to Nancy, the building's busy-body.

Not wanting to be seen, Paula stepped back into the stairwell, but not before signaling Nancy over the old lady's shoulder. Seeing her, Nancy hastily put an end to her conversation with the woman, claiming she was exhausted and needed to get back to bed. Nodding in accord, the nosy neighbor bid her goodnight and disappeared into her own flat. At that, Nancy looked towards the stairs and waved to Paula it was all clear. The statuesque brunette rushed along the corridor, and together they retreated into their own apartment.

"What's going on?" Paula asked the second they were inside. "I saw the police outside talking with Guler."

The pretty blonde was moving around the kitchen table, heading for the towel rack near the sink. "Porter Brewster, you know, the big guy who lives down on the first floor."

"Yes, he and my late husband use to work together down at the docks. He's a pig and treats his wife like dirt."

"Yeah, that's him alright." Nancy grabbed a blue dish cloth, put it under the faucet to get it wet, squeezed it, and then tossed it to her benefactor. "Here, you got blood all over your mouth and jaw."

"Thanks." Paula pulled out a chair and sat at the table, wiping the sticky red stuff from her face. "So, what's with Brewster?"

"He got fired a few weeks ago. Seems he's been hitting the bottle and missing work on a regular basis so they let him go."

"Serves him right."

"Maybe, but tonight he went out, got drunk, and came home late. When his poor wife starting ragging on him, he took his fists to her. Beat her pretty bad from the sound of her cries. Woke up the whole joint. Guler called the cops and, thank God, they got here before he could do any permanent damage."

Paula put down the now bloodstained cloth. "Is that coffee I smell?"

Nancy nodded and went to the pot by the stove. "When all the ruckus woke me up, I thought you might like some when you got home, so I put a pot on." She filled a white mug with the hot java and handed it over.

"Thanks." Paula took a long sip. "Hmm…good. So, I didn't see Brewster with the cops. Let me guess, Mrs. Brewster didn't want to press charges."

"That's what old lady Breinmer told me. She went down and listened to it all from the third floor landing. No surprise there. Like I said, they woke up half the joint.

"Anyway, by the time the coppers showed up, Brewster had passed out on the floor and his wife was nursing an ice bag on her eye saying she didn't want to cause no trouble. That her husband was just depressed because he lost his job."

Paula took another drink of the black coffee and then smacked her lips. "It's a tough world, kid. I feel sorry for Denise."

"Who?"

"Brewster's wife, her name is Denise. We've met a few times. She's not a bad person."

"Well she certainly doesn't deserve that kind of treatment, that's for sure."

"No, but people like them are old school, Nancy."

"What's that supposed to mean?"

Paula sighed. "You know, for somebody who lived on the streets as a hooker at such a young age, there's still a whole lot about this world you don't know."

"So, educate me."

"Didn't your old man ever knock your mother around?"

"My mother died when I was five. At least that's what I was told."

Nancy had never really told Paula much about her personal background, only that she came from San Francisco and had started turning tricks when she was sixteen.

"Oh...I'm sorry, kid."

"Hey, no big deal." Nancy found another mug and poured herself some coffee while she continued talking. "Apparently, my dad couldn't handle bringing up a baby on his own and ran out on me, which is how I became a ward of the state. I was raised in an orphanage, and by the time I was twelve, one of the male staff started coming around at night to bring me special gifts...because he...liked me."

Nancy added two spoons of sugar to her coffee, stirred it, and took a big gulp.

"And he..." Paula was having a hard time getting the words out. The lovely, outgoing girl had become a good friend to her in their short acquaintance.

"He raped me, Paula. No need to shy away from the word. It is what it is."

"Then what happened?"

"Of course, I told the headmistress of the place. She only slapped me across the face, called me a liar, and said if I ever repeated those charges to anyone, I'd be severely punished."

"What did you do?"

"I think I killed him, though I'm not exactly one hundred percent sure of that. You see, the day after my talk with the witch, I went to the maintenance closet where our janitor kept his tools and supplies. He had a hammer there and I borrowed it."

Nancy looked into her coffee cup as if looking into a black pool of divination. "I really don't know what I was thinking," she went on. "I just knew I'd had enough of the world crapping on me, and it was time to make it stop."

She looked up Paula. Her eyes were starting to tear up. "I hid it under my pillow, and when...Romeo showed up that night and got on top of me, I reached back, grabbed hold of it, and hit him in the side of the head as hard as I could.

"Oh, God, Paula, it made such an awful sound...like a watermelon smashing on the floor. He fell off me, and I got the hell out of there. I packed what little clothes I owned in a pillow case, including that hammer.

Then I emptied out his pockets and found forty-five dollars. It was enough for a bus ticket north...and..."

Nancy was crying now, one tear following another down her rosy cheeks. Paula pushed away from the table, came around the table and kneeling next to her, enfolded the wounded spirit in her arms.

Thus did the vampire console her dear, dear friend.

☻ ☻ ☻

Happily for Paula, the rest of the week was routine and uneventful. Her night job as a cigarette girl at the Gray Owl Casino went well with her enjoying the company of both her co-workers and some of the club's regular patrons. She especially liked flirting with the high rollers who were always leaving her generous tips, some naughtily stuffing hundred dollar bills into the top of her tight black bustier between the round naked tops of her breasts. As everything was all in good fun, she would play at slapping their hands away, calling them "bad boys" or simply "incorrigible."

The one sour note to these work hours was being around her ex-boyfriend, card dealer Blackjack Bobby Crandall. Sour because, as much as Paula had wanted the split to be clean and final, the sad look in Bobby's eyes every time they saw each other clearly demonstrated his inner pain. She'd broken his heart, and though he was always polite and cordial when they saw each other amongst the press of customers, she could almost feel his pain. Bobby had been there for her when her husband, Janos Wozcheski, had joined that monstrous cult that almost brought about her demise as a sacrifice to their unholy deity. It was the freckle-faced lad who had intervened by having Brother Bones investigate and ultimately save her life in the nick of time.

After Janos' death, Bobby had been her main source of strength and comfort. Eventually, their friendship had begun to evolve along a more romantic route. At least until she was kidnapped and turned into a vampire. From that point, Paula's only concern had been surviving, learning to adjust to her new existence, which left no room for anything else, including romance. By the time she began to truly adjust to her undead existence, she became conflicted in regards to her feelings towards Bobby. She still felt both a strong attraction to him and a true affection, but upon self-reflection, she realized there could never be anything more for them.

How can you love a vampire? A bloodsucking monster?

So, she had ended their relationship despite his pleas and protestations, letting him know in no uncertain terms they were finished.

But seeing him every night only served to rekindle buried feelings and make her question her decision. Yet she pushed those nagging doubts aside and continued to remain aloof. The sooner Bobby accepted the truth, the better it would be for both of them.

� ☠ ☠

Of course, the topic of domestic violence wasn't so easily shaken off, as Nancy Hansen continued to bring it up whenever she found some news story relating to the subject in the papers. She pestered Paula about the plight of all women in Cape Noire and how, in one fashion or another, they were second class citizens always at the mercy of men. Husbands beat their wives, single men cheated on their partners and, of course, the scumbag pimps lived off their stables of prostitutes who sold their bodies every night on the lonely, dirty streets of the great metropolis.

"So, what do you want me to do?" Paula all but screamed one evening after having endured the young blonde's repetitive, depressing tirade. "I can't save all the women in world, Nancy. I'm having a hard enough time taking care of the two of us."

"But you have all these wicked neat powers," the girl argued.

"Neat powers?"

"Well, you can fly. You have supernatural strength and you're impossible to...ah..."

"To what?" Paula challenged. "To kill. Is that what you were going to say?"

"Yes...well...sorta."

Paula slammed her fist on the small kitchen table between them. "Nancy, stop living in a fantasy world. Okay, so I'm a vampire and I can do those things you said. But I am not immortal. There are ways I can be killed, lots of them. Why do you think I invited you to live with me?"

"I know. So I could protect you during the day while you sleep and are vulnerable."

Paula Wozcheski pushed her chair back and stood. "Exactly. Because I am vulnerable fifty percent of every single day, Nancy!"

She started for her bedroom and stopped at the door. "I'm sorry, kid, but I am not some kind of avenging hero like Brother Bones. That's his gig in this cursed city, not mine. Can we let this thing go now, once and for all?"

Nancy was looking down at her feet, obviously ashamed. She raised her head slowly.

"Okay?" Paula repeated.

"Okay," Nancy mumbled softly. "I promise I won't bring it up again."

"Thank you."

Three days later Denise Brewster was murdered by her husband.

The bus dropped Paula off at the intersection a block from her apartment building. The minute she started down the street, she could see the lights of the police cruisers flashing and the ambulance, all converged in front of the main entrance. Several officers had placed themselves around the vehicles like a human shield to hold back the crowd of neighborhood people who were gathering.

By the time the tall brunette had reached the rear of the impromptu audience, two ambulance attendances were loading the cloth-covered body of Denise Brewster into the back of the white truck. Then, three big cops appeared at the top of the stairs dragging a yelling Porter Brewster down the stairs, his arms handcuffed before him.

"She had it coming!" he screamed at the onlookers, most were dressed in pajamas and other evening attire. Spittle flew out of his mouth, his eyes were bloodshot, and his face dirty and unshaven. "Always harping on me to get a job. Always calling me a drunk. So I taught her a good lesson, I did."

"Shut your kiester," the oldest of the policemen growled as they shoved him into the back seat of the nearest radio car. Once the door was slammed shut, the officers relaxed a bit. "Go on home now," the senior copper told the crowd. "There's no more to see here."

Heeding his words, the men and women began to shuffle away back to their own safe homes, many talking amongst themselves as they left, their voices buzzing away like the drone of insects. Some stepped out of the road as the ambulance, followed by the police cars, rolled away.

As Paula moved past the lingering stragglers, she saw Mrs. Guler leaning over her husband who was seated on the top step holding a bloody cloth to his head. Seated beside him was Nancy Hansen. She was holding a clean, wet cloth over the right side of her face. When she saw Paula, she rose to her feet and came down the stairs to meet her halfway.

"What the hell happened?" the vampire blurted, unable to hold back her own anxiety. "Did Porter do all this?"

Nancy nodded her head. peeling away her wet rag to reveal her left eye nearly swollen shut, bruised and purple. "About an hour ago he got home from some bar and he and Denise went at it again. Same old story. Then a little while later she started screaming. God, Paula, it was awful."

Paula held Nancy's chin and turned her face to the right to better examine her injured eyed. "Go on. What happened next?"

"Well, I knew this time it was really bad, so I ran downstairs just in time to see Mr. Guler come flying out their door. I guess he'd gone in there to stop him and Porter went nuts.

"Mrs. Guler was in the door to their place just wringing her hands and I told her to call the cops. Then I helped Guler to his feet.

"Denise screamed again, and this time the two of us went into their place. But by then it was too late. He...he..." The girl was having trouble as her mind replayed the horror she'd witnessed.

"Easy there," Paula soothed her. "Take your time. How did he kill her? With a knife or something?"

"No..." Nancy raised up her hands. "With his fists. He beat her to death. She was on the floor all broken up, blood all over her face. Porter had his back to us and when I yelled for him to leave her alone, he turned around and punched me.

"Somehow he and Mr. Guler went at it." Nancy looked towards the building superintendent with a half smile on her face. "I never thought he had that kind of moxie. At one point, they both fell down on the floor wrestling, and that's when I picked up this heavy kitchen chair and broke it over Porter's head. It knocked him out for a little while. Long enough for the cops to show up."

The girl sniffled, caught her breath, and finished. "But it was too late for Denise, Paula. She just died right there on the floor...and there was nothing we could do about it."

Paula opened her arms and embraced her distraught friend. "Come on, let's get you upstairs and see to that eye." She paused, looked at the Gulers and the remaining people on the street and said, "Then we need to talk."

☻ ☻ ☻

Twenty minutes later, Nancy Hansen was seated on her bed nursing a shot of whiskey Paula had poured for her from the bottle under the kitchen sink. She helped the girl strip and get into her nightgown and settled her in bed, propped up against several pillows. There she had washed her face with a clean wash cloth and applied some soothing antiseptic cream to the area around the swollen eye.

"I'm going to have a shiner, aren't I?" Nancy asked taking a small sip whiskey. She disliked alcohol and accepted the vampire's assurance it would calm her jangled nerves and help her relax. So far, the warmth in the belly was proving that true.

"Oh, yeah," Paula concurred sitting at the end of the bed. "But don't worry, I've had a few in my time and it will go away in a few days."

"You got punched around?" Nancy's exposed eye widened slightly. "You never mentioned that, Paula?"

"Look kid, it's an old world tradition. The man marries the woman. The woman becomes his property, and every now and then he has to slap her around to keep her in line."

"Did ...did your husband hit...ah...treat you like that?"

"Yes, he did. Thing is, I took it. I'm not proud of that now, looking back on it in hindsight, I can't believe I was that much of a coward."

"Then you agree with me it has to stop."

"I don't know, kid. You were right about Porter and now Denise is... well, I don't know. If I'd listened to you, maybe I could have saved her."

Nancy looked at the beautiful brunette and saw the regret in her face. Maybe she'd been too hard on her friend, but now was not the time to let up.

"It's not too late to save all the others, Paula."

"Please, we've gone over all ..."

"No, let me finish," Nancy pushed to her objective. "Paula, you can make a difference. You can help hundreds of women in Cape Noire by showing them how to fight back. By showing them how to stand up for themselves in ways they never had the courage to do before. You're the one woman in this hellhole of a city who can do it."

"Okay, okay," Paula was willing to give the idea a try. "So just how do we do that? I can't just suddenly appear in public and start murdering wife beaters."

"No, you can't. Which is why tomorrow I'm going to go shopping for you."

"Huh, shopping? Why?"

"Because Paula, like Brother Bones, you too are going to need a mask…a secret identity behind which to hide so that no one will be able to connect Cape Noire's avenging vampire vixen with Paula the cigarette girl."

"Wow, it sounds like you really thought this all out."

"Ha, yes, I guess I have at that. And you really are going to go along with this…for real?"

Paula Wozcheski nodded and smiled, "Yes, for real. Now it's time for you to get some sleep."

After taking the empty glass from Nancy's hand, she helped her stretch out under her covers, kissed her gently on the top of the head, and then exited her room shutting off the light switch as she did so.

Once in the kitchen she couldn't help but have one final doubt, *What the hell have I gotten myself into now?*

Paula Wozcheski slept every day from sunrise to sunset. Her vampire metabolism was so attuned to the cosmic forces of the universe that she did not require a mechanical timepiece to relegate her sleeping and rising. It was just after six p.m. when she opened her eyes from her dreamless slumber, yawned and tossed off her covers, then stretched her body like a cat, popping joints and limbering her muscles. She made a quick trip to the bathroom and then, donning her bathrobe, went into the cramped living room.

There she found Nancy Hansen toiling away at the old foot-pedal operated sewing machine in the corner.

Hearing her enter, the blonde looked over her shoulder, a dark purple circle around her left eye, and smiled as best she could. "Oh, hi, Paula."

Piled on the sofa in the middle of the room was an odd assortment of clothes and empty boxes. Paula walked over to it and asked curiously, "What's all this?"

"Your new costume," Nancy answered as she finished pushing a piece of deep red satin past her pistoning needle and pulled it free of the machine.

"My what?" Paula stifled a yawn and reaching down picked up a pair of knee-high shiny black riding boots. "Riding boots?"

She put them down and picked up a pair of khaki jodhpur-style pants. "Where did you get all this stuff?"

"The Five and Dime, and don't worry, you can pay me back later."

"WHAT'S ALL THIS?"

"Right, but you still haven't answered my question, Nance. Why do I need a costume?"

"Because, Paula, you just can't go out there and start killing off the bad guys without somebody eventually recognizing you. I mean, there are hundreds of people who see you at the club every night. Sooner or later, one of them will be able to identify you as Cape Noire's resident bloodsucker and the jig will be up."

As Nancy pushed her chair from the sewing machine, Paula reached down and picked up a beautiful red blouse resting atop a jet-black opera cape.

"This stuff is outlandish," she commented. "Even Brother Bones isn't this gaudy."

Nancy, carrying the strip of red satin in her hands, went over to the coffee table in front of the sofa and picked up an old magazine. She handed it to Paula. It was the latest issue of Captain Hazzard, the so-called Champion of Justice who operated out of New York City. His real-life exploits were chronicled monthly by writer Chester Hawks.

"Captain Hazzard? Really?"

"Look at his outfit, the boots, the jodhpurs etcetera. Only he doesn't wear a mask…being a public adventurer and all. I also bought some red dye and am going to dye those pants so they match the blouse. You'll be all red; except for the boots and cape, of course."

"And what about the opera cape?"

"Come on, Paula. You're a vampire. All vampires have to have a black cape. You know, to pull around their faces and hide themselves in the shadows."

"What's that in your hands?"

The blonde held up a long strip of sheer red satin three feet long and four inches wide. At the center she had cut out and fashioned two eyelets. "It's your mask. Here, put it on."

Paula took the thin, delicate cloth and hesitantly brought it up to her face so that the eyelets set around her bright green eyes.

"There you go," Nancy beamed. "Now just wrap the long ends around your head and tie them off."

Paula played along, knotting the silk behind her head, adjusted the cloth which now concealed the top half of her face and looked at her delighted roommate.

"Well?"

Nancy clapped her hands and exclaimed. "Hot damn, Paula! Hot damn!"

☻ ☻ ☻

Just past midnight, in another part of Cape Noire, the being known as Brother Bones sat in his padded chair looking out the window of his darkened room at the lights of the city. The former mob hitman, once called Tommy Bonello, never slept because he was no longer alive. He was a dead man animated by a power beyond human comprehension, forced to continue existence on this mortal plane as reparation for cruelty and pain he had made others suffer during his notorious career.

Thus he sat in his chair day and night, only leaving it when the fates that controlled his destiny summoned him through the ghost of the teenage prostitute he had murdered long ago.

It had been weeks since his last activity and when the slim candle set on the old bureau against the wall behind him flared to life, its shimmering flame snapped him instantly from his immobile status.

He clasped the arms of the chair and rose up; a tall, menacing bulk attired in a dark suit threadbare and torn. He moved over to the bureau, his dead eyes never leaving the flickering light. Beside the candle, on the dull wood surface, lay a gleaming white porcelain mask in the shape of a human skull, its smooth surface reflecting glimmers of the tiny flame.

Black dead eyes bore into that flame as a very familiar image materialized in its fiery yellow and orange tongues; it was the face of the lovely young girl.

"*Hear me, Brother Bones, another innocent one cries out for justice. A woman brutally slain by her own mate in a drunken rage.*"

The rotting, horrible face merely stared at the ghost's beauty. There was nothing new in her words.

"So where will I find this bastard?"

"*The police have him in a cell at the sixth precinct awaiting...*"

The ghost's face blurred suddenly and the dead man leaned forward slightly. That had never happened before. Something was afoul.

Then she appeared again, ethereal as ever but with a curious expression. "*A new player has entered the game.*"

"What's that supposed to mean? Who?"

"*Someone also seeking justice...a woman...a woman in red.*"

"What do you want me to do?"

"For the time being, nothing. Simply be aware of her actions and act as you will. The fates will support whatever your decide is best."

The candle sputtered out leaving Brother Bones standing in the dark again.

"Gee, thanks." He returned to his chair.

☻ ☻ ☻

Fighting crime was a full time job in a city like Cape Noire; in fact most of the men and women of the Cape Noire Police Department regarded their daily endeavors as containing outlawry rather than battling it. Fighting indicated a modicum of a chance for victory and in Cape Noire, no copper imagined such a possibility. The best they could hope for was to delay the tide of villainy enough to survive their twenty-years, grab their pensions, and move the hell out of there.

Thus, even at two in the morning, the main floor of the Sixth Precinct was a flourishing center of frantic activity as uniformed and plainclothes officers of the law came and went, chasing after one felony or another; all of which were phoned in to the communications office located on the first floor behind the duty sergeant's raised desk. Here three dispatchers, all males, answered call after call reporting witnessed crimes that demanded immediate assistance.

So it was that amidst this organized chaos of moving bodies, no one paid particular attention to the tall brunette draped in a black cape and wearing leather boots of the same inky hue as she wound her way past milling bodies to arrive at the base of the raised dais from which Duty Sgt. Perkins officiated.

He was giving a patrol officer a slip of paper on which was the address jotted down by one of the dispatchers. "Got us a breaking and entering, Andrews. Get on it!"

The young cop took the slip, nodded and spun off.

Perkins looked down and saw the masked woman for the first time. She stood before him, arms clutching her cape so that it enfolded her completely while she looked up at him through the red satin mask that covered the top portion of her face beneath her shoulder length dark black hair.

"Huh, whata we got here now?" he commented dryly. "A little early for Halloween, ain't it, deary?"

Now, this exchange didn't go completely unnoticed. Against the far wall sat two gaudily made up prostitutes in skimpy outfits puffing away on their cigarettes. They were handcuffed to the wooden bench on which they waiting to be booked and taken to the jail's holding cell. Both, bored out of their minds, had become alert upon seeing the oddly clad woman enter through the front doors and march up to Sgt. Perkin's perch. Each was watching intently as to what would transpire next.

"Where are you holding Porter Brewster?" Paula asked, straining to look up at the round-faced, beefy sergeant.

"Huh? Porter who?"

"Brewster. He is being held here for murdering his wife yesterday."

"Oh…right, that guy."

"Where is he now?"

"Who wants to know?"

"My name is unimportant. I'm here to punish him for his crime."

"I see." Sgt. Perkins had seen his share of nut-cases and it looked like he was about to add to that tally. "And just how are you going to punish him?"

"I would have thought that would be obvious." A small smile appeared on Paula's full, cherry red lips. "I'm going to tear off his head and drink his blood."

"Okay, that's about enough of that," Perkins raised his voice, leaning over the front of this station. He waved his right hand at two passing officers. "You…yeah, you two. Come over here…now!"

The two coppers shrugged and walked over to the dais, eyeing Paula curiously as they did so. "What's the problem, Sarge?" the older of the pair asked.

Sgt. Perkins, now having come to his feet, pointed down at the woman next to them. "I'd like you gentlemen to escort this weirdo out of here before I lose my sense of humor and throw her in lock up."

"Okay, you heard the sergeant," one of the two men said, turning to address the oddly dressed woman. "Let's go." He reached out to take hold of her arm.

Paula Wozcheski took a step backward, threw her cape open, and reached out suddenly to grab both men by the sides of their heads and, with one fast movement, slam them together. There was a dull cracking sound, and both men collapsed in front of her.

Sgt. Perkin's mouth dropped open.

Before he could close it again, Paula bent her knees and leaped up six feet into the air to land squarely on his desk. He fell back against his wooden chair with a scream.

By now, everyone one in the lobby had stopped what they were doing and turned to the commotion at the room's center. Those who had turned fast enough to see the caped woman fly up onto the top of the desk were stunned; frozen where they stood.

For his part, poor Sgt. Perkins very much wanted to scramble away, but he just wasn't fast enough. The red masked beauty simply bent over, grabbed him by the front of his shirt, and picked him up off his feet until he was dangling at arm's length above her four feet off the dais.

"Now, one more time," Paula growled, her top lip rising to reveal two sharp pointed fangs. "Where is Porter Brewster?"

"Ah…the holding cells," the scared man gasped.

Suddenly another male voice cried out. "Put him down, lady! NOW!"

Paula turned her head around and, looking down, saw a half dozen uniformed men below her, all holding their pistols and ready to fire, whereas all the civilians who had been crowding the floor minutes earlier were in the process of stampeding for any exit they could find.

"You want him?" The sexy vampire snarled. "Then you can have him."

She twisted her body and flung the sergeant down about his colleagues. Several coppers jumped out of the way, but the two fellows in the middle were not so lucky as Sgt. Perkins landed on top of them and they went down beneath his considerable weight.

"Open fire!" another officer yelled and instantly several revolvers began to blast away at the imposing figure above them.

Several bullets slammed into Paula and she screamed in pain. Angrily, she pulled her cape around herself and leaped into the air over the startled policemen to land only a few feet from the still handcuffed hookers.

Standing before them, she looked like a feminine fury personified.

"Where are these holding cells?" she asked them.

"Downstairs, in the basement," the prostitute with the curly red hair replied, pointing to the door down the hall to their immediate right. "That way!"

"Thank you," Paula said and then bolted off in that direction.

More shots were fired, most of them hitting the wall behind her as she raced around the corner. The first floor hall was filled with officers, most of whom were rushing towards the lobby having heard the gunshots, thus she was moving right at a wall of angry men, all with pistols drawn. Dropping her head, Paula plowed into them like a bowling ball scattering pins, her superhuman strength knocking the confused lawmen off their feet and sending them smashing into the corridor's walls to either side.

Then she was at the open door over which a plaque painted HOLDING

CELLS led to the stairs she was looking for. She all but flew down the steps, her black cape unfurling behind her like some flag in the wind.

At the bottom, to her left were the basement jail cells, six to either side of a long corridor. Near the landing was a small alcove where two guards were stationed. Both had been sitting around a small desk drinking coffee when the oddly dressed woman suddenly materialized before them. The one closest to door spilled his coffee all over his lap as he started to get up and reach for his sidearm. Even with the thick concrete walls all around them, the muffled gunfire had been heard.

Paula, moving like lightning, stepped into the tiny cubicle area and. picking up the stunned man, tossed him over the desk into his partner before the other could get out of the way. Both men tumbled backwards into a small cabinet where assorted cleaning materials were stored.

Satisfied they were out of commission for a few minutes, Paula turned her attention back to the cells and their occupants as she boldly marched down the center aisle. Her black riding boots beat a click-clack against the linoleum covered floor.

"Porter Brewster, I've come for you!" she called out. The first two cells she passed were empty. The second to her left held two shabbily dressed drunks, one asleep on his cot and the other sprawled out on the floor beside him. To her right, several gaudily dressed hookers were pacing back and forth like caged tigers. When one of them saw her, she moved to the iron bars that imprisoned them and gave her a curious look.

"Hey, sister, that's one bitching outfit," the prostitute said.

Paula ignored her for in the adjoining cell, seated on the cot with his back to the wall, was the slovenly Porter Brewster. He had just awakened from all the noise and was rubbing his eyes. Having spent a full day in jail, he was sober; something rare for the wife-beater.

Good, the vampire thought, *I want him to see what's coming!*

She stopped in front of the cell and took hold of the door just over the key lock.

"Who da hell are you?" Brewster spoke, his confused mind trying to comprehend what was happening.

"Get away from that door!" another voice called out. She turned to see three policemen at the foot of the stairs, all pointing their guns at her.

She smiled and pulled the entire door off its hinges. Everyone on the floor was stunned. "Holy crap!" gasped one of the hookers. Then Paula threw the heavy iron door at the cops. Forgetting to shoot, all of them tried to scramble out of the way of the rectangular missile. It landed at their feet as they fell over themselves in a panic.

Paula walked into the cold, bare room as Brewster jumped to his feet and tried to back away from her, an impossibility in the confined space.

Porter Brewster had been a bully his entire life, always picking on those weaker than he; always taking satisfaction in causing pain in those who were smaller than him. Seeing a woman rip the door off his cell as if it were made of paper immediately filled him with gut-wrenching fear.

"Hey...leave me alone!" he cried, fear etched across his unshaven face.

Refusing to expound any further dialogue with the killer, the dark-haired, masked beauty reached out her clawed hands and gripped him by shoulders. She slowly pushed him up against the hard wall, her long nails cutting into his shirt and the flesh beneath. He began to cry in pain, tears welling up in his eyes. His ineffective fists pounded feebly at her arms.

Then, the red masked vampire opened her mouth to reveal her deadly fangs as she struck. Her razor-like teeth ripped into Porter's neck and tore into it savagely. Hot warm blood spurted out of his ruined veins and artery and she drank it greedily. The man's eyes rolled up into their sockets and his bladder let go.

Without any thought of remorse, Paula continued to suck the copper tasting blood, its life-giving energy filling her with renewed vitality.

It only took her five minutes to drain her victim. Behind her she heard men approaching, and knew they had managed to get around the door she'd thrown in their path. Removing her mouth from the dead man's throat, the vampire reached up with both hands and with a loud twist tore his head off.

The two prostitutes screamed simultaneously.

Paula dropped the head on the floor next to where the body had collapsed. She turned and walked out of the cell to see at least ten coppers moving towards her. They were like frightened sheep, now clearly aware what they were facing was beyond their understanding or ability to deal with.

Paula's lower face beneath the mask was smeared with blood and gore. She reached up and wiped some of it off with the back of her sleeve then, looking at the approaching police force, smiled. Her white canines glimmered under the overhead light.

The cops all fired at the same time, and her body was hit with round after round, sending her reeling backwards. Yet she managed to keep to her feet until the barrage came to an end. Amidst the cloud of gun smoke, the vampire stood erect, though her blouse and cape were ripped and torn in several spots.

Her attackers looked on in utter disbelief.

Paula laughed at their impotence. Behind her, at the end of the aisle, was the fire exit door. Whipping her long cape about her, she twisted around like a ballet dancer and rushed the door. With one effortless kick, she popped it open and disappeared through it into the dark alley beyond.

The cops chased after her, but by the time they stumbled into the narrow black alley, there was no one there.

Then, from high above them, they heard a strange flapping sound.

☻ ☻ ☻

The following night, ace crime reporter for the Cape Noire Tribune, Sally Paige sat at her desk in the empty city room pounding away at her Smith Corona typewriter. She finished the final page of her story on the assault on the Sixth Precinct with typing in the number 30 below the last line.

With a flourish, she rolled the page out of her typewriter and set it atop the other two she had finished earlier. She pushed her swivel chair away from the black machine to center herself over the printed pages and brushed the back of her hand over her forehead wearily, moving strands of her black hair from her cheeks. Sally wore her hair long with a pageboy cut in the front. She was a beautiful woman without a hint of vanity in her body.

Being the only woman reporter on staff was a testament to both her tenacity and talent; being able to play rough and tumble with the big boys. Nestled between her scalp and left ear was a pencil, its surface chewed with teeth marks. She slipped it out of her hair with one hand while reaching out for her coffee mug with the other; time to reread what she'd just written and do some preliminary cutting.

Who-What-Where & When. The four Ws by which all good reporters lived. As her college teachers had instructed, everything else was unnecessary fluff. She took a drink from her cup and nearly gagged. The once hot java had gone bitter cold. Yuk. She put it down and took a deep breath while looking around the large, open city room with all its desks now empty. During midday the place would be an anthill of managed chaos with reporters, copy editors, secretaries, photographers and all the other vital personnel required to make a big city paper work properly. It was a world she loved dearly and one in which she was determined to leave her mark.

But now it was as quiet as the morgue downtown, with only old Bill Waters, the janitor, puttering around the washrooms at the other end of the floor out of sight in the darkness.

Normally, Paige would have been long gone as well, but when her editor, Hank Anderson, upon hearing about the police station incident, had sent her to get the "scoop" it had locked her in solid. Upon arriving at the Sixth Precinct, the savvy newshound had been given the cold shoulder treatment along with all the other reporters on the scene. Watching several ambulances carting off wounded policemen, it was obvious something truly extraordinary had transpired but, try as she might, Paige couldn't get one single officer to answer her questions.

By noon, an official department spokesman had offered the press a vague statement to the effect that sometime in the early hours of the morning, unknown parties had attempted to break out a prisoner. In the ensuing battle with the police, the prisoner was killed and the person or persons responsible for the attack had managed to get away. And that was it. Not another single word or extra detail.

Paige had started to walk away from the station in sheer frustration when a female voice got her attention. Standing across the street next to where she had parked her roadster were two women, prostitutes by their dress. One was a skinny blond and the other a tall, well endowed redhead. It was the redhead signaling Paige.

"Want to know what happened in there last night?" she asked when the reporter joined them.

"You know?"

"Honey, we were there from the moment that cape wearing bitch walked through the front doors." The redhead looked at her friend who nodded in confirmation.

"Wait, you say it was a woman responsible for whatever happened?"

"You got it, lady. She was something else…jumping around like some she-devil in her fancy red outfit and tearing into those blue-boys like they were little kids."

Sally Paige had heard enough. She pointed to a nearby café. "Okay, let's go in there and I'll buy you both breakfast and you can tell me everything you know."

Again, the two hookers gave each other a knowing look and this time the redhead said, "If you're willing to pay for it, that is."

Holding her purse against her side, Paige smiled not surprised in the least. No one did anything for free in Cape Noire. "Okay, I've twenty-five dollars for each of you if you'll tell me your stories. Fair enough?"

The redhead smiled. "Honey, you got a deal. Now let's go get that grub. Dottie and I got a real whopper you ain't gonna believe."

Sally Paige walked across the cavernous room towards the back wall table where the office help kept three coffee pots and pitchers of ice water during working hours. At night, the janitor kept one of the coffee pots filled for his own use and was only too happy to share with any of the staff pulling a late night assignment.

There was an open window to the right of the table, and Paige tossed out the dregs in her cup and then refilled with hot coffee. She ignored the sugar bowl as she preferred to drink it black, the caffeine helped keep her going.

As she started back to her desk, she reflected on how well Anderson had accepted her story after she'd returned from her interview with the two prostitutes. When one lived in a city where a zombie-like vigilante prowled the streets and rumors persisted of a gangland boss whose brain had been placed in the body of a gorilla, then the idea of a female vampire didn't seem all that farfetched. Anderson's only concern was that in writing the piece Paige was clear in delineating her information was provided by anonymous eye-witnesses, and that the paper itself offered no verdict on their testimonies one way or another. Only from that perspective would he allow her to write the piece and give it the next day's front page banner.

Paige understood where her boss was coming from but it still bothered her. She wanted something a whole lot more concrete to write; something solid that wouldn't read like some yellow rag exploitation piece. But having only hearsay information, there was nothing else she could do.

Lost in thought, the pretty newshound didn't realize there was someone standing in front of her desk until she almost bumped right into them.

"Hello," the tall woman in the red costume and mask said.

Paige's eyes doubled in surprise, taking in the black riding boots, red pants and blouse and the long dark opera cape. Still the most compelling sight was the satin mask wrapped around the woman's face.

"You're her!" Paige gasped. "The...ah..."

"Vampire who attacked the police station last night," Paula Wozcheski provided. "Yes, Miss Paige, that would be me."

"Ah...right." Frantically Sally Paige tried to compose herself. "What are you doing here?"

"I thought that would have been obvious, Miss Paige. I've come to tell you my side of the story. That is, if you want to hear it?"

☻ ☻ ☻

Paula knew there would be all kinds of repercussions once her interview with Sally Paige hit the street in the next day's morning edition. For whatever good or bad was wrought from her actions, the die was cast and couldn't be altered now.

Thus, when she arose from her sleep the next time, she went about her usual routine. Nancy had prepared a meal for her, and the two spoke briefly about the previous night's visit with the newspaper reporter. Although the blonde's attitude hadn't changed, her fervor was tempered by the reality that they had undertaken a dangerous course together and each was committed to seeing it through.

Paula was happy to see Nancy's shiner was healing, and before she left for the club, she gave the girl a big hug and kiss on the cheek.

"Everything is going to be fine," she said, hoping her words sounded convincing enough.

The crowd at the Gray Owl was bigger than normal that night, and she appreciated that because it kept her hopping all night long. She emptied the contents of her cigarette tray four times during the course of her eight hour shift, and her tight corset was stuffed with bills by the time she changed back into her street clothes before leaving. It was a nice haul that she neatly folded and slipped into the pocket of her worn topcoat.

The air was chilly when she came out of the club's back door and started out through the alley with several of her fellow workers. She was debating whether to take the downtown bus home or morph into her flying shape. Weary from the past few days, the slow bus trip seemed the best way to go.

She started down the street for the corner where the bus stopped every twenty minutes and saw a very familiar roadster parked across the street. Leaning against the front door she made out Blackjack Bobby Crandall, arms folded across his chest, smoking a cigarette.

Was he waiting for her?

"You changed the game," a deep, ominous voice said from behind her. One she recognized instantly.

Paula turned to see Brother Bones emerge from a tiny alleyway, his body encased in his black overcoat, his snow white mask half lost beneath the brim of his dirty slouch hat. His hands were holding a folded edition of the Tribune.

"I did what I had to do," she retorted, holding her ground as he approached her.

"I let you live with the proviso that you stay hidden, out of the spotlight…"

"And preyed only on the evil and the wicked. I haven't forgotten."

The grim Undead Avenger held up the newspaper and opened it showing her the banner headlines that visually proclaimed –

SISTER BLOOD
DECLARES WAR

"Is this your idea of keeping out of sight?"

Paula looked straight into Bones' black eyes. "No. But I can no longer sit on the sidelines while watching women all around me suffer every day."

"It is not your job to defend them."

"Then who? Yours?"

Brother Bones folded the paper and handed it to her. "That is not my mission."

"Right. So I've made it mine…from now on. Will you try and stop me?"

"No. For whatever reason, the fates have given your new role their approval."

"What's that supposed to mean?"

"That the powers that created me are aware of you, Paula Wozcheski, and for now, they choose not to interfere with this new path you've chosen."

Paula held the newspaper against her chest and continued to glare back at the frightening figure. "Nice to know, Bones, but I never asked for their permission. From now on I determine my own future. It's best you…and them…understand that."

"Then there's nothing more to be said," the black clad avenger nodded. He walked past her and started across the street towards the waiting Crandall.

Half way across the street, he stopped and looked back over his shoulder at her. "Sister Blood. Really?"

The tall, sexy brunette smiled for the first time. "Hey, just thought I'd keep it in the family."

Brother Bones shook his head slightly and walked away without another word.

Paula Wozcheski watched him and Crandall drive off just as the next city bus came around the corner.

She turned and hustled off to meet it. There was a lightness to her step.

THE END

THE GODLESS

Father Dennis O'Malley walked behind the two prison guards doing his best to keep up with them as they made their way down the corridor labeled Death Row. At the end of the hall, a young man named Darren Lassiter sat in his cell, counting the number of minutes he had left in this world.

The old priest had made these kind of visits often in his twenty years as the pastor of Saint Michael's Catholic church in Cape Noire. It wasn't unusual that men about to face the final unknown would grasp at whatever solace was made available to them. Death bed conversions, O'Malley called them; some were actually sincere, while others pathetic attempts to stave off the black void.

But it was not his place to judge. He was merely an apostle doing his best to fulfill his own purpose in this often cruel and savage world. Giving a frightened soul a tiny morsel of hope was never too much to ask, and although there were a million other things O'Malley would have preferred doing on this dark, rainy evening, here he was.

The two burly, silent guards reached the cell and stopped. One of them unlocked the door and stepped off to the side. Father O'Malley looked into the tiny square cell at the nervous young man with the long face and straw-colored hair that had been shaved close to the scalp. In minutes, Darren Lassiter would be strapped to the electric chair and ride the lightning, as the inmates described electrocution. His sentence carried out according to the dictates of the judge who had so ordained it.

Lassiter was seated on his bunk, his wrists and legs manacled. Fear covered him like a palpable scent and when he looked up at Fr. O'Malley, he looked like a beaten dog that had nowhere to run.

"The priest is here," the guard named Malone, rasped. He looked down at O'Malley and asked, "You want us to stay with you?"

"That will not be necessary," O'Malley said, clutching his prayer book to his chest. "It would be better if you left us alone together."

"Right." Malone indicated the open door and as the priest moved past him added, "You got ten minutes, father."

After they had relocked the doors, the two guards walked off. Fr. O'Malley stayed just inside the threshold afraid if he approached the skittish lad, he would only cause him more anxiety.

"Hello," he kept his voice soft. "I am Father O'Malley. They told me you wanted to speak with a priest. Is that true?"

"Uh-huh," the young man nodded. "I ain't got no religion. My Pa always said it was just make-believe to make suckers feel good."

"I see, and do you share his beliefs?"

"I don't know. Ma used to pray a lot before she died of cancer. But it didn't do her no good. She still died. Pa told us she was a fool like all the others. That there is no such thing as God."

"Then why did you ask to see a priest?"

"I don't know." Darren Lassiter ran a shaking hand through his uncombed hair. "I'm going to die and I'm scared. More scared than I've been in my whole life."

"And you didn't want to die alone, is that it?" The old pastor had seen this kind of all-consuming fear many times. It sucked all reason from a person's thoughts until they were completely helpless. It darkened the soul and robbed it of all life-affirming hope.

"I guess. Yeah...that's it, Father. I just didn't want to be alone anymore."

O'Malley pointed to the empty spot on the cot. "Do you mind if I sit down. These old legs of mine don't care for standing too long in one spot."

"Yeah, sure, go ahead."

The priest went over, turned, and sat down beside the convicted killer. He put his prayer book down on his lap and said, "If you don't want to talk, that's fine. We can just sit here and I'll pray for you in silence. If that's okay with you?"

Lassiter looked at the old man and nodded. "Sure. Go ahead."

Father O'Malley mentally began reciting the Lord's Prayer. He had gone through it twice when the young man spoke up again.

"Tell me about God," he asked.

☠ ☠ ☠

Sally Paige was one of two women in the witness room, which was nothing unusual in her line of work. As a crime reporter for the Cape Noire Tribune, the lovely brunette often found herself in male-dominated arenas of activity such as viewing a public execcution.

Seated around her were several of her colleagues from other papers and certain city officials. The other female was a middle-aged, gray haired soul seated in the middle of the group next to her husband who had one arm tightly wrapped around her shoulders. Piage recognized them immediately upon her arrival. They were Dave and Sue Collins. Their oldest son, Chase, had been one of the four armored car guards murdered by the Lassiter crew six months earlier. Witnesses had identified Darren Lassiter as one of the five men who had gunned down the guards after disarming them.

Mr. and Mrs. Collins were present to see justice meted out for their boy.

Paige had seen two other electrocutions, which was two too many. Yet when her editor, Hank Anderson, suggested sending another reporter to cover the event, Paige had shut him down. She'd been the lead writer on the story from day one, and was going to see it through to the bitter end.

As she fidgeted in the hard chair, she took out a notebook and pencil from her purse and started scribbling notes. It was her habit to jot down whatever details she absorbed, along with the reactions of her follow witnesses. Later, back at her desk, she would put everything together in what would be the next day's banner headline piece.

At exactly five minutes before midnight, the back door behind the dais where the wired chair was set opened and two guards appeared; Darren Lassiter, still in his manacles, shuffled between them. The last to enter was Warden Joseph Brown.

Everyone in the room stopped talking and a somber silence descended on them. The two guards methodically ushered Lassiter up the two steps to the platform and then around to the front of the electric chair. There, they removed his leg and wrist braces and sat him down. Working together, both men adjusted the leather straps that held the coils to his legs and arms, securing him to the chair.

Standing over by the electrical control panel, Warden Brown addressed the condemned man. "Is there anything you would like to say before your sentence is carried out?"

Sally Paige was holding her breath, gripping her pencil tightly, wondering if Lassiter would say anything. There was a strange expression of acceptance on his face, as if he was alright with what was about to happen.

Just then, Paige's eyes caught movement behind her and turned in time to see Father O'Malley come out of a side door. *Now what is he doing here,* she thought. The old white-haired pastor took up a position against the back wall so that he could see over all the heads looking directly at Darren Lassiter. Paige saw the priest was holding a leather-bound prayer book in his hands. She started scribbling in her notebook again.

Then Lassiter spoke. "All I want to say is…that I'm sorry for what I done." He was looking right at Mrs. Collins. "I'm sorry I killed your son. He must have been a good man…and…I hope he is in Heaven now."

Mrs. Collins started to cry and put her head into her husband's shoulder. Lassiter looked at the warden. "That's all I got to say, I guess."

At that, Brown nodded to Sgt. Malone and he lowered the metal head clamp to Darren's head making sure it was snug. Then, reaching into his back pocket, he pulled ,out a white cloth hood and carefully pulled it down over the convict's head. Lassiter's breath made the cloth over his mouth move in and out; his body began to tremble.

Paige looked back at Father O'Malley. His head was bowed and she could just barely hear him praying.

Back on the dais, the guards descended the stairs to stand by the control panel. Sgt. Malone took his place in front of the red handle switch. Beside him, Warden Brown held up his arm to look at his wristwatch, then he nodded.

Malone pulled the switch sending thousands of volts through Darren Lassiter. Lassiter's body bucked violently as he rode the lightning into death.

☻ ☻ ☻

There was a resounding boom of thunder as Sally Paige dashed across the open courtyard to the main reception area that faced the parking lot to the prison. Beyond this was a curving driveway that went out to the main highway and back to the city.

She pulled her jacket collar tight around her neck as rain lashed at her sideways from a strong night wind, making her wish she had worn a hat. Once inside the big, open, brightly-lit room, she shook her head like a dog flicking away the water from her hair.

Most of the other witnesses were going out the front entrance, and she spotted Father O'Malley waiting by one of the doors. She rushed over to him.

"Hello, Father O'Malley," she greeted. He was wearing a black, wide brimmed hat and a black overcoat.

He was surprised to see her. "Oh, Miss Paige. Hello." He glanced back toward the high gray prison walls behind them and understood her presence there. "Ah, you were sent here for your paper."

"Yes, I was," she confirmed. "It was you, wasn't it?"

"It was me…what?"

"It was you who gave Lassiter religion in the end. Wasn't it?"

"No one gives another 'religion' as you put it, Miss Paige. The boy asked to see a priest and I was summoned."

"So you what...heard his confession?"

"Hardly, and if I had, that would be confidential, as I'm sure you know." O'Malley was uncomfortable with the discussion. "If you don't mind, young lady, I'm waiting for a taxi that should be here in any minute."

"But you did talk with him, Lassiter, I mean?"

"Yes, that's what I said."

"Look, Father, I don't mean to be rude here, but Darren Lassiter is... ah...was a cold blooded killer. Just like his father, Deke. And up until a few minutes ago, back in there, he never once showed the slightest bit of remorse for what he had done.

"All of a sudden he's telling people he's sorry and contrite. C'mon, Father, my reporter's nose is itching like crazy telling me there's a story here, so why don't you tell it to me."

The old cleric smiled slightly. "I'm sorry, Miss Paige, but whatever happened to change that young man was none of my doing, I assure you."

"Meaning what, that God works in mysterious ways and all that stuff?"

"If you have faith, young lady, it's not just 'stuff.'"

Frustrated, Paige cut to the heart of the matter. "Can you at least tell me what you did talk about? That's all."

"We talked about God," the pastor said. "He asked me to tell him about God and I did." Then Father O'Malley looked out the window and saw a yellow Cape Noire taxi pull up to the curve. "Now if you'll excuse me, my ride is here. Good night, Miss Paige."

Watching the priest hurry out the door and through the rain, Sally Paige bit down on her lower lip lost in thought. If O'Malley wasn't lying, and she had no reason to believe he would do so, then whatever few words he and the late Darren Lassiter had shared had somehow worked a minor miracle. One she had witnessed with her own two eyes.

Paige pulled up the collar of her jacket again, tugged on her purse to make sure it was held in place on her shoulder, and then exited the building. As she raced in the rain to her parked sedan, all she could think about was getting back to her desk at the Tribune. Words and sentences floated around her thoughts, getting her more and more excited with each new phrasing she would pound out of her typewriter.

Oh, yeah, she mused, *Look out, Pulitzer, here we come!*

Being a port city, most of the commerce that kept Cape Noire humming was centered on its many docks. Being a deep-water port, the six mile long harbor area was always packed with foreign cargo ships from around the globe. Most of the cargo that arrived was kept in hundreds of giant warehouses stacked next to each other like a row of massive dominos. Many of the cavernous buildings were owned by criminal organizations and oftentimes provided safe havens for those on the run from the law.

Such was the case with Deke Lassiter, now going stir crazy in a top floor apartment building at the rear of one of these dirty gray warehouses. He and his two partners, Webster Headley and Rafe Neely, had been hiding out in the drab rooms ever since they had managed to escape a police raid at their former hideout; a small one story house on the outskirts of the city. The cops had hit the place early one morning, obviously having been tipped to where the gang was holed up. Seeing they were outnumbered, Lassiter had ordered them to bust out the back door and make their way through the back alleys behind the neighborhood. They had managed to do that, shooting several coppers in the process, and then they had split up, each of the four going off in a different direction.

It wasn't until two days later when they all met up at the warehouse rendezvous that Deke Lassiter learned the police had caught his son, Darren.

Of all the rotten luck. Still, he had assured both the black-skinned Neely and the sadistic Headley that his boy would never rat on them. They were safe as long as they stayed cooped up and only ventured out at night, and then only to get needed supplies.

Thus, the intervening months crawled by at a torturous snail's pace for the three killers, but none suffered more than the gray-haired, big man, Deke Lassiter. The thought of his only son rotting away in jail drove him to the bottle with a dire resolve. When they heard the news of Darren's conviction and subsequent sentencing over the small radio they had, Deke, in a drunken stupor had punched holes in the wall until his fists bled.

Both Headley and Neely continued to keep him supplied with cheap whiskey, and watched silently as he set about drinking himself to death. Lassiter lost weight, his once square face became thin and brooding. His gray beard grew wild, as did his mop of hair, until he was no better than a street bum. The two gunmen began talking about simply shooting him some night when he was passed out and fleeing with the loot they had taken from the armored car heist.

The problem was neither man was more than a thug, both having dropped out of grade school and between them there wasn't enough intelligence to fill the head of dog. Without Lassiter to lead them, they were nobodies and they knew it. Thus, reluctantly, they had stayed with him, hoping that eventually something would happen to shake him out of his fugue so that he could once again plan out their next move.

That moment arrived the day after Darren Lassiter was executed.

It was early afternoon, the sky over Cape Noire was a cerulean bright blue after the previous night's thunder storm. A few puffy white clouds hung over the Pacific, and gulls cried loudly as they scoured the docks for edible refuse spilling out of trash containers.

Rafe Neely, dressed in his tee-shirt and pants, was playing solitaire in the main room while listening to the radio. Deke Lassiter was asleep in one of the two bedrooms, loudly snoring away through the open door. Webster Headley had gone out to buy some cigarettes, beer, and a local newspaper.

When Headley came through the front door, one arm holding a paper bag with smokes and booze, he looked frantic. In his hands was a rolled up edition of the Cape Noire Tribune.

"Where's Deke?" he asked stupidly when Neely looked up from his cards.

"Where da hell do you think he is?" the black man said, indicating the bedroom with a nod of his head. "Something wrong?"

"I'll say." Headley put the bag down on the table and handed his friend the paper. "Check out the headline."

Neely put down his cards, opened the newspaper, and saw the big blocky type that stated, ELEVENTH HOUR CONVERSION. "What does that mean?"

"Go on and read it," Headley urged while he started for Lassiter's bedroom. "Hey, Boss, you gotta wake up and see this."

With only a third grade education, Neely could just barely make out the article under the headlines. Still, he could understand that it told of Darren Lassiter's death on the electric chair, and then there was a lot of other stuff about a priest that he couldn't decipher at all.

Meanwhile, Headley had managed to awaken Deke, who was now grumbling to be left alone.

"But you gotta see what's in the papers," the stooge persisted. "It's about your boy, Darren."

"Darren? Huh, what about Darren?"

"Please, Boss, come see the paper. Neely's got it in the other room."

There was some shuffling and then Deke Lassiter, holding onto the doorframe, emerged looking like something the cat had dragged through every back alley in Cape Noire and then dumped into a sewer. The emaciated Lassiter ran a hand through his thick, grimy hair as his beady eyes tried to focus on Neely at the table.

"What you got there?"

"It's the Trib," Headley provided coming up behind Lassiter. "It's about Darren. Right there on the front page."

At that, Neely folded the paper and held it out to Lassiter. Swaying on his feet, the mobster reached out and took it. Slowly, he opened it. The words were blurry, but he kept squinting until they began to take solid shape.

As he began to read, the words slid like venomous snakes into his mind. His blood began to race throughout his body, boiling up a seething anger from deep within until everything before his eyes was red.

They had killed his boy.

Deke threw the paper away, grabbed his temples and falling to his knees, screamed for all he was worth.

They had killed his boy!

☻ ☻ ☻

When he was a young seminarian, Father Dennis O'Malley always complained about getting up early for the six o'clock morning mass. One of his teachers, an eighty-year-old Jesuit, upon hearing his complaint one day, assured him that the older he became, the less sleep he would require no matter what the circumstances.

After all those years, having himself become a pastor well on in age, the priest often remembered with fondness those words of wisdom. Time had indeed worked its wiles on his body so that now he actually relished rising before daylight and saying the early morning service. In fact, as he stood at the podium before the altar of Saint Michael's about to read passages from the Lectionary, his thoughts marveled at the irony of it all. This was by far his favorite mass of the day.

Seated behind him, his blond-haired altar boy, Billy Carpenter, tried to stifle a yawn by burying it in the voluminous sleeve of his cassock. O'Malley smiled.

Only the most devout of his congregation had the fortitude to attend thus the six o'clock service never had more than ten to fifteen attendees; most of these either seniors or laborers, most from European countries who still carried on the traditions of their parents, starting each new day with worship.

Adjusting his reading glasses, Father O'Malley opened the big book and his fingers touched the words as he began to read from the gospel of St. John. "I am the good shepherd: the good shepherd giveth his life for the sheep."

There was suddenly a loud banging from the front entrance as if someone had shoved the doors open hard. Then, out of the shadows of the vestibule, Deke Lassiter and his men appeared. All of them wore topcoats and fedoras and each held a gun.

"Bah…baah…baah, you sheep," Deke said loudly and then held his gun up in the air and fired a shot.

The sound reverberated throughout the church and several women screamed, others crossed themselves clutching their rosaries.

In one of the pews towards the back, a middle-aged man in dungarees started to run for a side exit door. Rafe Neely shot the man in the back. The man cried out and collapsed behind the wooden pews.

"STOP!" Father O'Malley shouted as he stepped away from the podium and pointed an accusatory finger at Deke Lassiter. "In the name of God, who are you and what do you want here?"

"Who am I?" the gaunt criminal repeated, tapping his chest with his .45. "Why, I'm Deke Lassiter, that's who I am. I'm the father of that kid you bamboozled up at the prison two nights ago."

O'Malley studied the sick looking man but couldn't see any resemblance with the boy he'd comforted. "I don't understand."

"Well, let me make it crystal clear to you, padre." Lassiter swung around and pointed his gun at an old woman wearing a cheap cotton shawl draped over her head.

Fear was evident in her face as he leaned in closer. "You. What are you doing here?"

Barely able to speak, the parishioner, Maude Lewis, mumbled, "I come to pray."

"Ah, you come to pray. So you believe in God do you?"

The woman's throat seized up and she couldn't speak.

"ANSWER ME!" Lassiter yelled in her wrinkled face. "DO YOU BELIEVE IN GOD?"

"Leave her alone…" Father O'Malley started rushing down the three steps to the floor of the nave.

Deke Lassiter turned around and shot him in the shoulder. O'Malley was thrown on his back. Seeing O'Malley gunned down, Billy Carpenter cried out, "Father O'Malley!" and ran to his pastor.

Before he could reach the fallen cleric, Deke shot him in the chest.

Then, Lassiter turned back to Mrs. Lewis and shook his head negatively. "Sorry, grandma, there ain't no freaking God." He pulled the trigger and blew the top of her head off.

Through the piercing pain in his shoulder, Father O'Malley managed to lift his head up. His glasses had slipped part way off his face and with his hand trembling, he reset them. What he saw was the towheaded boy lying next to him, dead. A huge pool of dark red blood was pooling over the boy's white vestments. covering the mark of the cross.

Dear God, save us. He prayed silently and then, in Latin, he mentally offered up the prayers of Last Rites for the innocent boy who was so dear to him. Tears flooded his eyes.

"So what do you think now, priest?" Deke Lassiter asked, a sadistic smile on his face as he waved his smoking gun over his head. "If there is a God, then how come he doesn't come down here right now and squash me like a bug? Huh? How come he doesn't come down here and save all your stupid asses?"

Lassiter moved away from the pews and looked down at O'Malley. "Sheep, ain't that what you was reading, heh, padre?"

"You will pay for your crimes," O'Malley managed to gasp. "No one escapes His judgment…either in this world or the next."

"Ha, ha, ha, ha, you people are the worst flim-flam artists of all." Lassiter looked out at the remaining parishioners, some now on their knees, their lips moving in fevered, silent prayer. "Making these poor saps think there's something better. That there's a God who loves them while they spend their lives scraping for every penny they can find and in the end still die with nothing.

"You religious fools make me sick." With that Lassiter bend down and spit in O'Malley's face. "You're just a bad joke!"

He pointed his gun at the priest and then laughed again. "Naw, killing you would be too easy. You just bury these fools of yours and know it was you that got them killed."

Lassiter walked down the aisle without a backward glance at the wounded priest. "Come on, guys, let's go grab something to eat. Shooting holy-rollers gives me a wicked appetite."

💀 💀 💀

It was two hours later when Sally Paige and Tribune photographer John Finlay arrived at Saint Michael's church in Finlay's green sedan. A group of uniformed officers were dispersing the gathered crowd at the bottom of the cement steps and several ambulances were driving off down the street.

Thick clouds covered the city, setting the tone for what would be a gray and somber day. Paige was barely awake, having been sent out only a few minutes after she'd arrived at her job. She hadn't even had a cup of coffee yet, and that in itself was guaranteed to put her in a foul mood.

As she and Finlay walked across the street, she recognized a few other newshounds from rival papers trying to interview a young priest. She recognized him as Father Janus Cominski, the Assistant to Pastor O'Malley. At first ,Paige intended to jump into the conversation, but at the last minute she spotted Detective Lieutenant Dan Rains over by a black and white radio car.

"Get a few shots of the priest and the church," she told Finlay. "See what they're saying."

"Where you going?" the camera-bug asked as she started off in the opposite direction.

"I just spotted a better source."

Lt. Rains, a tall, muscular fellow with a chiseled, handsome face, was leaning over the passenger door, the radio mic from the dashboard in his hands. She heard him sign off and hand the mic to the patrolman behind the wheel.

Dan Rains turned, sighted Sally Paige and made a face.

"A sunny hello to you as well," Paige, greeted. "So, what's the scoop? My boss said there was a shooting here? Is Father O'Malley alright?"

"He took a slug in the shoulder," the veteran investigator said. "They rushed him down to Saint Mary's. Medics said it looked like he would be okay."

Paige had her notebook out and was scribbling away. "Damn it. And I just saw him a few nights ago."

"Yeah, where?"

"At Darren Lassiter's execution."

"Well, that explains that." The brunette stopped writing and looked up, wanting him to go on. "Those witnesses who escaped said there were three shooters and the one in charge called himself Deke Lassiter."

Rains reached into his pocket for a pack of cigarettes. He flipped one out and offered the pack the Paige.

"No, thanks. Are you sure about that, I mean, it being Deke Lassiter."

The detective pulled out a lighter and lit the tip of his cigarette. "The people we talked to all said the same things and their descriptions do fit Lassiter. They said he was ranting about his boy being fried and how he hated O'Malley for making the kid a wimp before he died."

"Huh?"

"One of the women said Lassiter was nuts, screaming there was no such thing as God and then he just started shooting people."

"People…as in plural?"

"Yeah," Rains eyes reflected a deep pain. "Beside O'Malley, they shot an altar boy, an old lady, and some fellow who worked as a butcher down on Ralston Street. They never had a chance."

Sally Paige stopped writing her notes. "Jesus, Rains. In cold blood?"

The copper nodded and blew out a puff of smoke. "I'm wondering if that piece you wrote might have set off old man Lassiter."

"You mean my story about the execution? How do you figure that?"

"Well, you laid it on pretty thick about the kid's sudden turnaround, saying he was sorry for all the bad he'd done. I'm thinking if Lassiter saw that, it might have been the spark that set him off."

The reporter felt as if she'd been punched in the heart.

"Hey, are you alright, Paige?"

"I changed my mind, Rains. I'll take that cigarette now."

The detective handed her his pack and pulled out his lighter again. He could see Sally Paige was more than a little upset.

As he torched the end of her cigarette, he said, "Hey, forget I said anything. Okay?"

"I wish I could," she replied, inhaling deeply. "Oh, God, this is just nuts."

"No, Paige," Rains snapped his light shut. "This was murder. It's Deke Lassiter that's nuts."

Later that night, in the bedroom of a dingy apartment, a candle wick spontaneously flamed up, creating a soft, yellow glow that did little to dispel the room's inky darkness. The long, skinny candle rested atop a four-shelf bureau and beside it, on the polished surface, rested an ivory white face mask in the shape of a human skull.

Seconds after the flame appeared, squeaking noises arose from the chair set facing the window. A tall, silent figure stood up from that padded seat and, turning his gaze away from the city's skyline, he turned to the tiny firelight.

It was his calling from the beyond and his sole reason for being. The once living mob killer walked over to the bureau and, standing before it, stared into its sparking, yellow and orange light.

The Undead Avenger known throughout Cape Noire as Brother Bones watched the dancing flame with cold, bottomless eyes. He felt nothing; he knew no excitement or anticipation as he was incapable of such, these being human feelings and he was anything but human. Bones existed for only one purpose, to answer his summoning and mete out retribution accordingly.

From within the flickering flame, the image of a lovely young girl appeared. She was his spirit guide; the messenger from the fates that had cast him into his undying role. This time she was not alone, for just as her face materialized before him, Brother Bones felt the room's temperature fall and then three ghostly figures were seen floating over the bed behind him. One was a young teenage boy wearing an odd uniform of some kind. Behind the ghost boy was a very old woman and, next to her, a sad-faced man with a hard, square, unshaven face.

"Billy Carpenter, Maude Lewis and Karl Wandoyski," the spirit guide said in a soft, melodic voice. "All of them were taken from this world early this morning while at mass."

"Mass?" The dead man's voice sounded like gravel scraping together. "They were killed in a church?"

"Saint Michael's," the lovely vision continued. "You know it well, don't you, Brother Bones?"

"That's Father O'Malley's church." There was no concern in his words. He simply stated the things he knew.

"The old priest was shot but will recover. But these three souls have been taken from their loved ones and need to move on."

"Who did it?"

"He is called Deke Lassiter."

"I know the name."

"Then find him and deliver your justice."

The three levitating ghosts moaned softly and then, with arms outstretched towards Brother Bones, they melted away. The candle flame flickered again and then went out.

In the darkness, cold, hard hands reached out and picked up the white porcelain mask and carefully placed it over the ruined landscape that was Bones' dead flesh. Infused with magic, it required no cord, and when he pulled his hands away, the skull mask remained in place.

"ALL OF THEM WERE TAKEN FROM THIS WORLD EARLY THIS MORNING WHILE AT MASS."

Then Brother Bones opened the top drawer of the bureau and from it pulled out two silver plated Colt .45 automatics and slipped them into the twin shoulder rigs under each arm.

It was time go hunting once more.

☻ ☻ ☻

Now, it would have been impossible for a creature like Brother Bones to function on his own in a metropolis like Cape Noire. The sight of a black-clad, mask-wearing undead zombie walking the streets would never have gone unnoticed, and his sacred mission would have ended in its infancy. What Bones required was a living assistant, and he had found such in a freckled-faced, red-headed card dealer named Blackjack Bobby Crandall.

Crandall had almost become collateral damage in a vicious gang war between two rival mobsters, Topper Wyld and Big Swede, both now deceased. It had been the supernatural arrival of the Undead Avenger that had saved Crandall's life, and from that moment on he had served Brother Bones faithfully, albeit reluctantly at first. It was in Bobby Crandall's flat that Bones resided, and it was the kid who drove him to and from his death-dealing rendezvous with the worst monsters the city had to offer.

Over the ensuing months, Crandall had come to respect Bones' crusade until he began to willingly take a more active participation in what had evolved into a strange but true partnership. In return, though he was incapable of displaying emotions, the Undead Avenger had acknowledged the lad's contribution by widening the scope of his responsibilities. Without ever saying the words, it was clear that Brother Bones respected his assistant and had come to rely on him without hesitation.

Of course, even despite this adjustment, Bobby Crandall's life was no less weird. It wasn't enough that he was allied with a supernatural force of justice which constantly put his life in jeopardy but in the past several months Crandall had fallen in love with a gorgeous brunette who also worked at the Gray Owl Casino. She was a very sexy cigarette girl and the sight of her in fishnet stockings and a tight black bustier was enough to make any man's heart beat faster.

Paula Wozcheski had been the one normal thing in Blackjack Bobby's chaotic world. Then, she was bitten by a vampire, and in turn became one. Now, to his credit, Crandall was willing to accept the woman's cursed situation, much to her stunned surprise. Up until that point, Miss Wozcheski hadn't realized just how much the kid truly loved her. Whereas, she too had valued his affection, she couldn't see any way their relationship could continue without invariably harming him; either physically or emotionally.

Paula dumped him. End of story.

Or so she said.

Crandall would never accept that, and seeing her every night at the club without being able to talk to her was pure torture. Yet he resolved to do whatever it took to prove to her she was wrong. No matter how long it took.

These were the same thoughts swimming through his mind that night as he drove home after a long shift at the casino. It was almost one a.m. and he was tired. All he wanted to do was wash up, crawl into bed, and get some sleep.

As he pulled up to the side street alongside his apartment building, a tall shadow wearing a large slouch hat stepped off the curb right in front of him. Crandall slammed on his brakes, his headlamps coloring the ghoulish visage of Brother Bones in a sick yellow.

"Crap!" he cursed as his zombie boss moved around the car and entered on the passenger side.

"I have a new mission," Bones spoke, closing his door. "Take us to the Gridiron Saloon in Old Town."

Easing off the brake pedal, Crandall shifted down into first gear, drove to the end of the street, and turned right.

"Let me guess, this is about the shooting at Saint Michael's."

"Yes. The dead call me to avenge them. One was an altar boy, the others…"

"I know, Bones," Crandall cut him off. "It's been the talk all over town. They say it was Deke Lassiter and his boys."

"Yes, Lassiter was the shooter. Tonight, he will face justice at my hands."

With the lateness of the hour, the streets were empty and Bobby Crandall continued talking so as to stay alert. "Okay, this really doesn't surprise me. When I first heard of what happened, I thought you might get a call from your spirit angel."

Brother Bones kept looking forward as if he wasn't listening to the driver.

Crandall kept up his chatter. "But it got me to thinking about something."

"What?" the cold voice asked.

"Well, why didn't this angel spirit, or whatever she is, come to you months ago when Lassiter and his gang hit that armoreded car and killed those four guards? I don't get why she didn't send you out back then. I mean, if she had, then you'd have killed them all and they wouldn't have been around to go after those folks in the church."

As they rolled down the eerily deserted streets, the only sound was that of the car's motor purring and the tires humming over the asphalt. Crandall had no idea how Bones would respond to his query. Or if he would at all.

Almost five minutes elapsed before the grim masked avenger turned his gaze on Blackjack Bobby. "I don't know, Bobby Crandall."

Crandall turned his head for a second peering into dead eyes. "Really?"

"That is not my job, to choose who lives or dies. Which bad guys I go after. That is decided by..." Bones seemed to be fumbling for words. "By those who made me...like this. Who sent me back to be their weapon of justice."

Slowly, Crandall turned his gaze forward again. "That's all I am, a weapon used to avenge the innocent. Woe to any who cross my path."

☻ ☻ ☻

"All right you moochers, last call," Butch Hammer barked to those remaining patrons in his Gridiron Saloon. "One more round and then out you go!"

A tough guy, Hammer had been a professional athlete before joining the U.S. Marines during the Great War. He'd returned home a decorated war hero with a nice bankroll which he used to open up his watering hole. A small, clean establishment in the heart of Cape Noire's Old Town, Gridiron Saloon was also a local hangout for some of the city's more notorious citizens.

Hammer had no problem with crooks and hookers as long as they behaved themselves while in his place. If they did not, he either kicked them out onto the street with the use of the baseball bat stowed under the bar or, if things got dangerous, he'd whip out the sawed-off shotgun instead. As most of his customers knew about his exploits in the trenches, none of them were foolish enough to challenge his ardor. Butch Hammer would not hesitate one second to blow a hole in someone if that someone threatened his customers.

Which was why he was personally stunned when the front door opened and the black dressed specter walked in. Hammer had never laid eyes on

Brother Bones before, but he recognized the white bone mask immediately. He moved to the end of the bar where he kept his shotgun.

The Undead Avenger, his gloved hands empty, simply walked past the empty booths and up to the bar. There two of the remaining drinkers saw him and wasted no time downing their drinks and scrambling for the exit. The third, too drunk to know any better, looked Bones up and down and then smiled before going back to his half-finished beer.

"What do you want?" Butch Hammer put one hand on the stock of his weapon while facing the creepy figure before him. The gut-tightening fear he'd known back in the killing fields of France came back to him like a familiar but unwanted memory.

Brother Bones looked around the bar and spotted a small man seated in the last booth near the rear door. As the rat-faced fellow hood pushed his fedora back on his head and looked up, the Undead Avenger raised his hand and pointed.

"Him," Bones said. "I've come for Reed Vengel."

Like a greyhound racer coming out of the starting gate, the wiry Vengel bolted out of his booth and ripped open the back door disappearing into the alley.

Brother Bones started towards the door calmly, his hands loose at his sides.

"Hey, spook," Hammer warned. "I don't want no trouble."

"Then mind your own business. I only want to talk with the bum." That said, Brother Bones walked out the door.

He found the little man on his back with Blackjack Bobby Crandall standing over him. A single streetlamp at the end of the alley provided just enough light to show the horror on Reed Vengel's pointy face.

"Look who tripped over his own two feet," Crandall said, indicating the fallen crook. The young card dealer had recognized the fleeing man as one of the mobsters who had been responsible for his abduction at the hands of the late Jack Bonello. The diminutive felon had fled the scene when he and his companions had been set upon by the wraith of Tommy Bonello. Because of that, Blackjack Bobby had been the only witness to the macabre metamorphosis that transpired that night. He alone had seen the ghost of a dead man invade the body of his murderous twin brother to become the Undead Avenger.

This was the first time Bobby Crandall had seen the mousy Reed Vengel since that fateful night. Considering what was happening, he was not surprised that the crook didn't recognize him.

"What do yah want with me?" Vengel cried waving his hands in front of his face in a feeble attempt to ward off the grim figure towering over him. His voice was breaking as if he was about to start weeping.

Brother Bones reached down, grabbed Vengel's jacket with both hands, and lifted the small man into the air. Effortlessly, the Undead Avenger held the squirming gangster off the ground so that Vengel's twisted face was only inches from his own masked visage. Vengel couldn't look into the cold black eyes that bore into him.

"Noooo! Don't kill me!"

"You once were a part of Deke Lassiter's crew," Brother Bones said.

"That was long ago," Vengel.

"Tell me where he is…"

"How should I kn…"

"And I will spare your worthless life," Bones finished.

Reed Vengel gulped. It was getting hard to breathe.

"I will not ask again. TELL ME NOW!"

"Alright, alright. He has a pad over a warehouse by the docks. Number seventy-three. It's on Boyson."

For a few seconds Brother Bones remained stock still, his grip tight on the scared Vengel. Then he released him and Vengel fell to the ground at his feet.

Without another word, Brother Bones turned and, nodding to Bobby Crandall, they left the alley and the whimpering Reed Vengel.

Bobby Crandall puffed on his cigarette as he watched Brother Bones vanish behind the massive, time-worn gray warehouse that was their target destination. He ran a shaking hand through his rust-colored hair nervously. The drive from the Gridiron Saloon to the harbor district had been thirty minutes and, according to Crandall's wristwatch, it was just after two a.m.

As he smoked, he could hear the lonesome sound of a ship's foghorn wailing off in the distance far beyond the outer banks of the bay. He had never been to sea ,nor did he have any wish to do so. There was something unnatural about being surrounded by hundreds of miles of water, vulnerable to storms and such. Never mind whatever beasts resided in the furthest depths beyond the light of day.

Blackjack Bobby had been forced to read "Moby Dick" while in school and the thought of a giant leviathan swimming just beneath the waves had given him nightmares. The horn sounded again, and Crandall took another drag on his cigarette.

He still couldn't believe running into Reed Vengel after all this time, or that the little slimeball had failed to recognize him. Life sure had a way of doubling back on itself. If Brother Bones had not materialized on that long ago scene, he would have died and his own remains most likely been dumped in the harbor behind him.

Instead, he had survived and, like the Bonello brothers, he, too, had been transformed. Blackjack Bobby Crandall would never be a victim again. Imagining his boss climbing the back stairs to the hidden loft atop the warehouse, Crandall saw Bones as another land predator, his white skull mask reflecting the same doom as Melville's white whale.

And he, Bobby Crandall, now swam with the biggest shark of them all; Brother Bones.

☠ ☠ ☠

Brother Bones held his automatics pointed straight ahead, set himself squarely in front of the wooden door at the top of the stairs behind the building, and then, bringing up his right foot, kicked it open.

The lock snapped off as the door swung inward to reveal only darkness.

Brother Bones laughed a twisted, horrible sound as he stepped into the room. Whatever light from the stars above filtered in behind him and he was able to make out a man rising up from behind a small card table to his front.

Rafe Neely had fallen asleep playing solitaire. Now, crudely snapped out of his pitiful dreams, he looked upon the ghoulish face of Brother Bones. On the table among several empty beer cans was his own pistol. He clawed for it while the angel of death laughed.

Bones' .45s boomed in the confines of the apartment and four slugs tore into Neely kicking him off his feet and backwards over the folding chair he'd been sleeping in.

As the black man's body hit the floor, Webster Headley came charging out of the main room, blasting away with his own gun. Dressed only in a tee-shirt and boxer trunks, he emptied his entire clip into the human fiend with the skull face.

Each piece of hot lead slapped into Bones and rocked him, but he neither cried out nor fell. Rather, he took each shot until Headley's gun clicked empty. The killer looked down at the now useless weapon and then back at the undead vigilante.

Brother Bones laughed again, lifted his right hand, and squeezed off a single shot. The bullet hit Headley between the eyes and plowed out the back of his head, spraying blood and gore everywhere. The gangster folded over like a ruptured balloon.

Bones waited. Where was Deke Lassiter? Why hadn't he attacked?

Knowing no fear, Brother Bones entered the apartment moving quickly, by now the starlight had given everything around him a grayish outline. He could make out a second bedroom and what looked like a tiny kitchenette. As he started to step over the fallen body of Rafe Neely, a scream erupted from behind him.

Brandishing a huge butcher knife, Deke Lassiter sprang out of the tiny kitchen and drove it into Bone's back almost to the hilt.

Brother Bones took two stumbling steps forward almost slipping in Rafe Neely's blood. Lassiter waited for him to fall over.

But he did not.

Steadying his feet, the towering masked zombie slowly turned around to face the sadistic murderer. As Lassiter looked at Bones' mask, he saw the eye slits appeared empty as if void of anything. Then, Bones stepped up to him and two black orbs were suddenly visible to the killer.

Brother Bones shot Deke Lassiter in the stomach. The gangster fall back against the card table and, unable to hold on to it, fell to the floor onto his side.

Bones came over and, using his foot, pushed Lassiter onto his back. The criminal was clutching his bleeding stomach and grimacing in pain. "Go ahead, do it! Finish me off!"

"No," Bones said. "Not before you are shown the error of your ways, Deke Lassiter."

The Undead Avenger put away his guns and then dropped to one knee beside the mortally wounded Lassiter.

"You say there is no God," Brother Bones continued without emotion, his voice calm and steady. "No Heaven or Hell."

"Yeah, so what?" Lassiter groaned. "It's all bullshit. There ain't nothing after death."

"Wrong, Deke Lassiter. There is good in this world and there is evil. There is a Heaven and there is a Hell."

With that, Brother Bones bent down closer to the dying man and removed his ivory mask. In the dim light, Deke Lassiter saw his face and began screaming. He screamed until his sanity was lost and there was nothing left.

And still he screamed…

� ☙ ☙

Father Dennis O'Malley found sleeping with his tightly bandaged shoulder a nearly impossible thing to do. Lying with his back slightly raised up in his hospital bed, he was lucky to doze off for a few hours before his body became uncomfortable and brought him back to wakefulness. Thankfully the pain medicine worked.

Opening his eyes for what he thought might be the third time that night, he shifted his body slightly and looked up at the ceiling tiles. A tiny night light was plugged into the wall next to his bed to facilitate his being able to call a nurse should the need arise.

He'd been in the hospital three days, and already he was feeling like a prisoner anxious to go home to his rectory at Saint Michael's.

There was a soft sigh, and the old pastor sensed he was not alone. There was somebody else in the room with him.

"Please come out where I can see you," he spoke to the black spot in the far corner opposite the room's door to the hall. "Or else you're liable to scare me into having a heart attack."

"You need not fear me, padre," a chilling voice replied.

Brother Bones stepped out of the blackness to stand at the foot of O'Malley's bed. For a second the priest caught his breath at the fearsome sight of his visitor. In his pajama shirt pocket was a rosary which he now took hold of with his good arm.

"Who are…wait." A look of recognition crossed the priest's face. "Brother Bones. It has been a while since your last visit…about the Golem, I believe."

"Yes, and thanks to you, that matter was resolved without any further loss of life." Bones kept his hands to his sides. "I am sorry about what happened to you."

"No one ever said being a priest would be safe," Father O'Malley smiled weakly. "You're the last person I would have expected to pay me a visit here."

"The lessons I was taught in the monastery have never left me, padre. In part I do owe you that."

"Is any part of the young man I once advised still in you, Brother Bones? I've always been curious about that. It's difficult to tell beneath that grotesque mask you wear."

"Maybe a small part, padre. But I really don't know anymore. I've become something else. An instrument of vengeance."

"I know. I'm sorry, my boy. That is not what I wanted for you."

"Sometimes our choices are few," the dark figure said. "Had I not taken up this role, then there was only the abyss before me."

"Why are you here?"

"To tell you that Deke Lassiter has been dealt with and will never again hurt another soul in this world."

"Meaning you killed him." There was a genuine sadness in the priest's voice. "That is not my way. Not the faith I practice."

"No, it is not. You are a good man, padre. Each of us has a mission in this world that may one day usher us into the next."

"Do you truly believe that, my son?"

"I've seen His light, priest. I know it is real...though I may never experience it for myself."

"Then I will pray for you."

"If you wish. Just know this, in the end we both confronted godless men. You were responsible for showing Darren Lassiter the way to the truth and maybe saved his soul in the process."

"And you?"

Brother Bones moved away from the bed and over to the door. He took hold of the silver knob and then looked back at Father O'Malley.

"I showed Deke Lassiter ell...and then I sent him there."

Father O'Malley whispered a prayer and closed his eyes. When he opened them, he was alone and his night caller gone.

THE END

EPILOGUE

Four days after he was murdered, young Billy Carpenter was laid to rest in Saint Michael's cemetery located out in the northern tip of the city limits. The twenty acre expanse had been donated by a wealthy parishioner during the early days of Cape Noire's history. The hilly, manicured fields with their stone and cement markers were dotted with small copses of evergreens which provided some areas with cooling shade.

Three hundred members from Saint Michael's community had attended the requiem mass officiated by Father Janus, the assistant pastor. The other two victims in the horrible church slayings had been memorialized in services the previous day. None of these had been as crowded as that of the young fourteen-year-old altar boy.

Sadly, Father O'Malley was still recovering and was unable to attend to any of these services. Instead, rosary beads in hand, the old priest had offered his morning vespers from his bed to the eternal repose of a boy he'd grown quite fond of. Tears glistened over his cheeks as he prayed in silence. When one of his floor nurses walked in to check on his vitals and saw his sad face, she immediately spun around and exited.

After the funeral service for Billy Carpenter was concluded, sixty automobiles joined the motorcade to the cemetery on that peaceful, warm and sunny Wednesday morning.

Among those gathered around the gaping hole covered with a green felt cloth to hear final prayers were Billy's family; his parents and an older brother and sister. Behind them were aunts and uncles, cousins and neighbors, school chums and many parishioners who hardly knew the boy at all. The people of Cape Noire were not strangers to violence, but when it struck down one so young, then they responded. Something this vile made them interrupt their daily routines and come out and pay their respects to the family in mourning, all the while praying such a horror never befell their own.

Along with these good, hard-working people were several members of Cape Noire's elected officials, including the councilman who represented the district in which the Carpenters resided, the district attorney, a few members of the police department, and, of course, the agents of the press.

Birds fluttered overhead and their songs seemed to blend in with Father Janus' gospel words, "Ashes to ashes, dust to dust…"

And then it was over and slowly the family of Billy Carpenter bid their last farewells and departed. The crowd began to move away back to the side road where the hearse and the other vehicles were parked. Over by a city police cruiser, reporters had surrounded the District Attorney and were peppering him with questions concerning the increase of violence and how did civil authorities plan on dealing with the situation.

Reporter Sally Paige remained at the grave site, looking at the two coverall-wearing workers who were getting ready to start filling in the hole over the casket as soon as everyone was gone. She could see her colleagues flocking around the D.A. and hear their inane questions. It seemed cruel somehow. The poor kid had just been interred and just like that it was back to business as normal in Cape Noire.

"Shouldn't you be up there with them?" Lt. Dan Rains asked as he appeared next to her.

She shook her head negatively. "I can't shake the feeling I had something to do with this. You know, my piece about Father O'Malley might have been the spark that set off Deke Lassiter and led to..." She pointed to the grave because suddenly she couldn't speak.

"Stop it, Sally," Rains said forcefully as he took hold of her elbow and turned her to face him squarely. "I've talked with Father O'Malley and we both know that isn't true. Deke Lassiter was a savage animal and he alone is responsible for this. No one else!"

Sally Paige's eyes started to moisten. She wanted to believe Rains more than anything in the world.

He opened his arms and she accepted his embrace as she began to sob.

"Geezuz, Paige, when are you going to stop being so hard on yourself?"

☻ ☻ ☻

"The following program is a rebroadcast of a show that was recorded earlier."

He hunts the fiendish, evil forces bent on destroying the city he loves! The makers of Wyld Ale are proud to present The Wyld Ale Mystery Hour featuring the Avenging Angel of Cape Noire, BROTHER BONES!

Starring Preston Elliot as Thomas Bonaparte, a wealthy playboy who, when donning his eerie white skull mask, becomes the scourge of criminals everywhere, the mysterious vigilante Brother Bones.

With Flora Reynolds as Dinah Rogers, his lovely companion, Bruce

Mallory as Lawyer Conrad Huntley and Steven Traynor as the loyal, street-brawling taxi driver, Gus.

   And I am your announcer, Donald Mayer.

Tonight's story – **THE DEVIL'S BRIDE!**

Part one begins after this quick word from our sponsor…

Click!

Bobby Crandall shut off the radio on the kitchen counter and lit up another cigarette. The wall clock told him it was after two in the morning and he knew getting any sleep this night would be a lost cause.

It had been this way for the past few days; ever since Bones had gunned down Deke Lassiter and his men. Normally, after such a victory, Crandall had no trouble getting back into the normal pattern of his life, if one could ever describe being the ally of an Undead Avenger normal. The truth was he had long ago accepted his role in Brother Bones' crusade and no longer had any problems with it.

But now, for whatever inexplicable reasons, the freckle-faced card dealer found himself cursed with insomnia.

He started to pour himself another cup of coffee until he realized the pot was cold. He'd already had four or five; he'd lost count. For the past two nights, he had come back to his apartment after work, washed up, and climbed into the bed only to remain wide awake staring up at the ceiling and thinking about the past few weeks.

The same thoughts spun around in his mind like a crazy carousel as he saw Bones relentlessly pursuing the scum of Cape Noire while he rode along with him. He saw Paula Wozcheski telling him over and over that they were through and nothing would ever change that. In the end, he got out of bed, went into the kitchenette to pour himself a drink, read the papers, listen to the radio or play a hand of solitaire. But the images wouldn't go away until he thought he was losing his mind. It was as if all of it had soured his life and nothing mattered any more.

Wishing not to repeat the drawn out agony of the past two nights, Bobby Crandall threw on his jacket and left his apartment with no plan in mind other than to just get out. Thankfully, since the Lassiter mission, Brother Bones had been silent, locked away in his solitary room. For that, Crandall was most grateful.

Until he got this insomnia thing worked out, the last thing he wanted was to go out on another of the Undead Avenger's weird assignments.

Stepping out onto the front stoop of his apartment building, he found the night air pleasant and decided against taking his roadster. He took a final drag of his smoke, tossed the butt away, and started down the sidewalk.

Walking along, he felt himself relax. *Maybe it's just cabin fever,* he reasoned. Maybe all he needed was just to get out by himself.

Considering the life he led, his social activity was a flat out zero. Especially after Paula had dumped him. Thinking of the beautiful, leggy brunette only made him bitter again and he picked up his pace. He remembered there was an all night movie house only a few blocks away. Maybe a cheap picture and some popcorn might get his mind on something else. What the hell, it was worth a try.

Crandall was totally unaware of being followed as a shadow moved along the nearby rooftops parallel to his path.

The Bijou, as advertised, was still open and Crandall slid a quarter under the glass partition to the half-asleep plump girl who had been doing a crossword puzzle when he stepped up. She tore off a ticket, slipped it to him, and then went back to her puzzle.

Then he found the refreshment lobby deserted with no one manning either the popcorn and candy counters. The redhead merely shrugged and went on through the swinging doors that led to the darkened theater beyond. It was only as he was walking down the carpeted aisle that he realized he hadn't even bothered to look at the marquee posters to see what was playing.

On the giant silver screen was the black and white scene of an open desert and a bobbing stagecoach was being chased by a group of masked outlaws; all firing away with their six-guns. The noise from the wall speakers was loud and abrasive, but Crandall didn't care. A mindless western shoot'em up might be just what the doctor ordered.

As his eyes adjusted to the darkened interior, he counted no more than five other people, all men, scattered throughout the huge theater, a few looking to be fast asleep in their seats. With any luck, he might soon be one of these slumbering souls.

He stopped half-way down the aisle, walked along the empty row and sat himself down in the middle of the hardback seats. Stretching out his legs as best he could, he folded his hands over his body and sat back to watch the movie.

By now, the outlaws had managed to stop the stagecoach and were in the process of ordering the helpless passengers out. They had already shot the guard who had toppled off the fast-moving coach in a spectacular

Hollywood death-dive. Now, only the old, grizzled driver remained, and of course he would be of no help to the passengers about to be robbed.

Any moment now, the dashing hero should come riding over the hill to save the day, Crandall mused, having seen the same scenario a hundred times or more in movie palaces such as those back home while growing up. Even as hokey as it was, he still loved cowboy movies. Maybe because most of them were so simple; a good guy, a bad guy and you always knew how it would come out in the end.

Whereas real life never followed the script you had in mind.

Sure enough, the picture's stalwart hero had just ridden onto the scene, riding his magnificent white stallion, when Crandall caught a movement to his left. Someone in a long, slim overcoat was moving down the aisle towards him.

What the hell?

Paula Wozcheski moved quickly seating herself next to him and before he could fully comprehend what she was doing, she brought her hand up and put her index finger over his lips.

"Shhhh," she whispered. Her eyes were so bright; they glimmered reflecting the glow of the giant movie screen.

She removed her finger, leaned into him, and brought her lips down on his lips. The kiss was long and tender, the feel of her lips stirring his emotions. Then she forced his mouth open and their tongues mingled. In the process, Crandall's brushed over her long, pointed incisors.

The feel of the vampire's fangs was an entirely new experience for him and, rather than dissuade him, it only served to excite him more. His mind was flooded with the memories of their past lovemaking sessions and he couldn't help but wonder what it would be like to make love to her now. Would it be tempting fate? Would, in the heat of passion, she be tempted to…bite him?

Paula broke the kiss and pushed away from him. "No," she said softly. "Just hold me, Bobby…please."

Words caught in his throat, he nodded, bringing his left arm up and around her shoulder so that she could rest her head against his chest. "Yeah…" he finally said. "Okay, Paula. Okay."

💀 💀 💀

Two hours later, Crandall woke up alone to a new feature playing on the big screen.

Had he dreamed Paula's presence? Had she really been there? He started to brush his hand through his hair when his tongue tasted a small trace of lipstick still there. He touched it gently, smiling, more mixed up than ever.

But still, he smiled.

☻ ☻ ☻

It was a cold day in Cape Noire, and Reed Vengel clasped his ragged coat tighter while holding on to his hat with his other hand as a gust of wind tore at him. Despite the sun's appearance, the northern blast from Canada was sweeping through the city, sending millions of pieces of junk and debris everywhere. Men and women who had to be out and about struggled against the powerful winds.

Rushing to turn a corner in the hopes of escaping that pulling force, he plowed into a tall, unmovable object and nearly fell off his feet.

"Hey, get out of the freakin'..." He looked looked up and up and up at the biggest, tallest black man he had ever seen.

Mr. Garrett reached down, grabbed Vengel by the neck, and then half dragged him across the sidewalk to the parked Duesenberg. He opened the back door and threw the little, rat-like man into the car and slammed the door shut.

Vengel, unable to utter a single word in his own defense, found himself lying across the back seat next to Alexis Wyld. A one-time member of Topper Wyld's army, he recognized the cold, cruel beauty who now glared at him stoically.

"Miss Wyld...it's you!"

"Yes, Mr. Vengel. How observant of you."

"Ah...what's this all about?"

The new boss of the Wyld crime syndicate opened a small black hand purse and from it took out several hundred dollar bills. "I am told you are in need of funds. Is that true?"

"Well...sorta. I've fallen on hard times, yah see..."

"Be quiet. Your sordid affairs do not interest me in the slightest," she sneered and then handed him the two bills. "Here, take this."

"Ah...what for...Miss Wyld?" Vengel was scared and confused.

"I want you to tell me everything that occurred several weeks ago."

"Huh?"

"During your encounter with Brother Bones. I'm told he confronted you one evening at the Gridiron Saloon. Is that true?"

"Ah…yah…he did."

Alexis Wyld glared at the dirty crook like a cobra eyeing a mouse.

"Tell me everything you know about Brother Bones, Reed Vengel, and do not leave out a single detail.

"I want to know everything!"

FINIS

MORE BROTHER BONES....

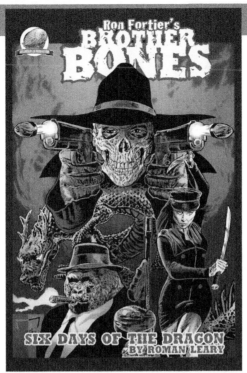

RON FORTIER'S DARKEST CREATION RETURNS!
WHEN THE SOULS OF THE INNOCENT CRY FOR
JUSTICE, *ONE MAN* HEARS THEIR CALL:

THE UNDEAD AVENGER--BROTHER BONES

HE STALKS THE STREETS OF CAPE NOIRE, WAGING A NEVER-ENDING WAR AGAINST THE FORCES OF DARKNESS. BONES HAS NEVER MET A FOE HE COULD NOT DEFEAT, BUT NOW HE FACES AN ENEMY UNLIKE ANY HE HAS EVER KNOWN. WITH ONLY A MOTLEY CREW OF UNLIKELY ALLIES -- AND HIS SILVER-PLATED TWIN .45S -- BONES MUST STOP AN ANCIENT EVIL THAT THREATENS NOT ONLY CAPE NOIRE, BUT THE ENTIRE WORLD.

SIX DAYS OF THE DRAGON

BROTHER BONES IS BACK TO CUT A SWATHE OF DESTRUCTION THROUGH HIS FIRST FULL-LENGTH NOVEL! WRITER ROMAN LEARY AND ILLUSTRATOR ROB MORAN DELIVER THE GUN-BLAZING THRILLS IN THIS EPIC TALE OF TWO-FISTED ACTION AND SPINE-CHILLING HORROR!

Nominated for 5 Awards!
New Pulp Awards: Best Cover; Best Interior Art
Pulp Factory Awards: Best Novel; Best Cover Art; Best Interior Art.
See what everyone's raving about!

PULP FICTION FOR A NEW GENERATION!
CHECK AIRSHIP27HANGAR.COM FOR AVAILABILITY

Airship 27 Productions
NEW PULP

THE UNDEAD AVENGER
BROTHER BONES

GRUESOME IN ANY FORMAT! NOW AVAILABLE IN COMIC BOOK AND AUDIOBOOK

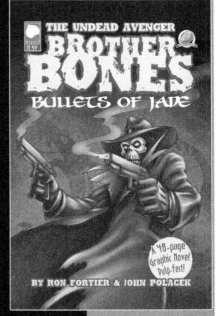

FIND THE LINKS FOR THESE AND OTHER NEW PULP CREATIONS AT AIRSHIP27HANGAR.COM!

PULP FICTION FOR A NEW GENERATION!

AN AIRSHIP 27 PRODUCTION

NEW PULP